The Land

of

Whoo

Enjoy the Land of Whoo!

Ryan O'Brien

Ryan O'Brien

i

www.TheLandOfWhoo.com

This book is a work of fiction. Names, characters, places and incidents are the product of the author's imagination or are used fictitiously. Any resemblance to actual events, locales, or persons, living or dead, is coincidental.

This book is dedicated to Erma,

our True North and guiding light.

CONTENTS

CHAPTER 1

A NEW BEGINNING

It was a sunny, yet cool, morning in June when Michael Henry woke up with a start from his vivid dream. In his dream, he had seen a messenger bathed in a white light. He was very tall, around seven feet, muscular and bald. His appearance reminded Michael Henry of a genie.

The strange messenger relayed a directive to Michael Henry without talking. The messenger advised him that he had been selected as the Chosen One for his time, and that he would be given important instructions to be followed precisely in the very near future.

Wow! Michael Henry knew he had a very vivid imagination and thought perhaps a comic book he had been reading in bed before falling asleep the night before might be the reason for the dream. Yet he had a ping in the back of his mind that the messenger would be back.

Somehow Michael Henry felt out of place. Like a cold bean in a hot bowl of chili or a mother who had lost a child, he knew something was missing in his life. But what was it? Could this dream be a harbinger of things to come, or was it really just a dream?

He had a big day planned. His school was out for summer break, and he was going to explore his new neighborhood on his bike. He felt like a ship without a rudder. He was drifting away from his best friend, Xavier. Almost all of the friends he had been close to in his former upscale neighborhood were now hours away from his new house.

Michael Henry's dad, Dan, had been without a full-time job for the past two years, ever since the economy had gone downhill and his construction and remodeling business had gone under. Michael Henry's mother, Samantha—or Sam, as everyone called her— was a nurse who worked in a downtown Seattle dialysis center. Michael Henry could see it in his mother's face when she lost a patient. She said it was like losing a close friend to the inevitable.

Dan and Sam had just moved into a thirty-year-old, broken-down house after they'd lost their dream home through foreclosure. They'd been unable to keep up with the payments after Dan lost his business. Dan was heartbroken and felt like he had let his family down when they had to leave their old neighborhood, yet he knew he had worked very hard over the years to provide for them. And after all, most of his friends in construction had also suffered from the hard blows of the economy.

Michael Henry's family had been in their old beater house two weeks. Michael Henry had been able to attend a new school, the Academy, on a two-week trial at the end of the school year because the principal was so impressed with Sam's passion for her son's education. Once Michael Henry had been accepted, the principal told Sam that there were scholarships available that they could apply for to help with tuition.

Dan had just landed a two-week job working for a roofing company. He knew Michael Henry missed his old friends, even though he thought Xavier was a bad influence on his son. Dan told Michael Henry it was fine to go exploring in his new neighborhood, but to keep his phone handy in case he was needed. Michael Henry packed a crunchy-peanut-butter-and-strawberry-jelly sandwich, filled his water bottle, and headed out the door.

Sam and Dan had been fighting every night behind closed doors, both wanting the best for their two sons but not agreeing on how to accomplish such a large task. Michael Henry's older brother, Jeremy, was attending Whitworth, an expensive university across the state in Spokane. Jeremy knew it was a hardship on his parents and was having thoughts about enlisting in the Army as a way not only to help his country, but to pay for his schooling.

Michael Henry left to explore on his own. He was getting away from it all, riding hard on a lonely, winding road on the outskirts of Marysville. He was approaching a gate when a girl waved to him. "Hey, Michael Henry, what are you doing here?"

He looked at the strawberry-blonde girl with the long wavy hair. He recognized her from his two weeks at the Academy. He sheepishly approached her. No matter how hard he tried, he could not remember her name.

He needn't have worried. The girl stood by her rural mailbox and greeted him. "I'm Savannah James from the Academy. We're all glad you joined our class this year. GiGi and I just made a batch of peanut butter cookies, hot out of the oven. Come on and join us!"

Michael Henry thought homemade cookies sounded awfully good, especially peanut butter ones, so he answered, "Okay." Savannah got the mail out of the mailbox, and they headed for the house. She walked him to the farmhouse where she lived with her grandmother and her mother. She loved GiGi, which was short for Grandma Gloria, and spent many happy hours with her. It sometimes seemed that her mother, Leslie, was always gone, either working or with her

3

new boyfriend, Paul. Savannah told Michael Henry she had always enjoyed long walks with GiGi on their forty-acre farm. As they walked, Savannah was happy to have company. She told Michael Henry that her father had left when she was five years old. Michael Henry wanted to tell her that he was adopted and that his real mother's name was Marie, but something stopped him. All he knew about his birth mother was that she had died at a young age and the angels had carried her to heaven.

Michael Henry enjoyed the delicious cookies and the cold milk, yet he sensed that GiGi was holding something back. He wasn't sure what he felt about his new friend and her grandmother, but he would find out GiGi's secret soon enough.

His thoughts were interrupted by the vibration from his phone. It was a text message from his dad. "Hope u r having a great day. Let's meet at 4 and work on the yard to surprise Mom when she gets home. Love u, Dad."

Michael Henry relayed the message to Savannah, and she rode her bike with him to the main road. They traded phone numbers and away he went. After all that had transpired, he noticed that his water bottle and sandwich were still on his bike. He rode off, waving to the girl with the wavy, strawberry-blonde hair, blue eyes, and warm smile.

He got back home just before Dan arrived from his backbreaking day at work. "Okay," said his dad, "let's get started on the yard." This was the first nice day outside, and Dan wanted to take advantage of it. Most of the boxes and furnishings had been unpacked and put away inside. Now it was time to get the yard in order. Dan thought of his former house with the immaculately groomed yard in the upscale neighborhood. Trees had framed the stone walkway to the fountain in the backyard where Michael Henry had liked to hang out with his friends. Dan reminded himself once again that that was then and this was now. The two worked together on cutting the grass and removing all of the debris that had collected in the yard during the two years that the house had been vacant. They continued without any breaks until around 7:00, when Sam's white minivan pulled into the driveway.

"How was your day, Mom?" asked Michael Henry.

She said she'd had two new patients who had just started on the program and that it had been an exhausting day for her. Then she looked around. "Wow, guys, the yard looks amazing! Let me admire it for a while." Dan and his son went inside to start dinner. They were having pasta, one of Michael Henry's favorites. After dinner, he got a text from his older brother, wondering how his first day of summer break had gone. Michael Henry texted back, "Met a girl from my new school on a bike ride. Think she likes me. Xavier thinks I should run away back to the old gang for the summer."

Michael Henry read a few pages of his comic book and then drifted off to sleep. He awoke to a vision of the messenger from the night before, communicating with him with a confident and smiling face. Without uttering a word, the message came to Michael Henry in a crystal-clear directive: "Michael Henry, Michael Henry, you are indeed the Chosen One for our time. Tomorrow the Medallion will make itself known to you. Follow the instructions from the envoy exactly. No deviations. The lives of others are at stake. Savannah will lead you to the entrance. Take an LED flashlight with you. Once inside, find the Whoo Portal. Shining your light will illuminate the portal. When the portal is illuminated, repeat the following exactly as I tell you. The portal will ask, 'Who are you?' You must answer, 'Michael Henry, the Chosen One, and Savannah James.' Entrance will be allowed immediately."

Suddenly the picture frames moved, dogs barked, and sirens wailed as the walls shook in the sturdy thirty-year-old house. Michael Henry was uncertain if he was still dreaming or if the vibration was real. His dad rushed into his room to assure him that everything was okay, reminding him that they lived on a fault line. Dan turned on the radio and learned that there had been a minor tremor. He told his son that he was confident the old house was up to the stress, so all was well. "Go back to sleep, Michael Henry. There's nothing to worry about."

When he awoke in the morning, Michael Henry was still in awe of the dream and the messenger. He was anxious to see what possible adventure this new day might bring. He walked into the kitchen and had his favorite breakfast, Honey Nut Cheerios and toast with strawberry jelly. Mom and Dad had left him a note that they were both working and to pick up his room before he went exploring today. He spent a couple of minutes partially cleaning his room and then off he rode on the same path as yesterday, his mind racing as fast as he was pedaling. How would he be contacted? Would they be able to find the opening? What was happening? He hoped he would find out some answers soon. He put his hand in his left pocket to make sure he had remembered to take his flashlight.

He arrived at Savannah's mailbox again, but no Savannah like yesterday. *What the heck,* he thought, *why not text her?* He pulled out his phone. "R u home today? Going on a bike ride and passing by. MH."

No sooner had he sent it than the girl with the long, wavy, strawberry-blonde hair texted him back. "Coming to front gate to let u in. Don't go away pls."

Wow, that was fast. A few minutes later, Savannah was riding her bike to meet him at the road leading to her house. She was already talking to him as she opened the gate. "What a night we had last night, Michael Henry! The earthquake had all the animals very uneasy. GiGi wants me to ride my bike on all the trails to be sure everything is okay. I was

6

going to text you to come and help me but…but…hadn't yet. Can you go with me to look around after we have lunch?"

"Sure."

Leslie, Savannah's mom, had been called in to work at the medical clinic, along with all of the other nurses. The extent of damage from the quake was unknown. It would take everyone to help verify that all was up and running to handle the many patients coming for treatment today. It was just Savannah and GiGi at home, along with Savannah's Golden Retriever, Penny, who was always excited to meet new people. When Michael Henry had visited the day before, Penny had been with Leslie for her annual visit to the vet for heartworm pills and vaccinations. He was surprised to see the dog bounding towards him, all eighty pounds participating in the licking and tail-wagging excitement. He had to be careful so she didn't knock him and his bike over.

Michael Henry greeted GiGi as they walked up to the house. She seemed very different from yesterday's visit. Her eyes were red and swollen. He wondered if she had been crying but was afraid to say anything. Savannah dished up a lunch of venison chili that was left over from dinner last night. While heating the chili in the microwave, Savannah put Fritos in the bottom of a bowl. She added the chili and sprinkled shredded cheese on top. She told Michael Henry that the venison had been a gift last season from her uncle Tim, who was quite the bow hunter.

It was still brisk outside, and the chili felt good as Michael Henry devoured two big bowls along with four homemade rolls. He was thinking about a third bowl when Savannah's voice interrupted his thoughts. "Let's get going, Michael Henry, and help GiGi rest assured that her animals are fine."

GiGi had the news on. They heard the news anchor say there had been only very slight damage from the earthquake the night before. *Great*, thought Michael Henry, *his dad would be able to continue working on his roofing job.*

GiGi told them to be careful and to take Penny with them for company. The dog ran ahead on the cattle trails, as happy as any retriever had ever been, with Savannah and her new friend, Michael Henry. All looked good on the front half of the forty-acre farm, so they stopped for a rest and some water from a clear babbling spring alongside the trail.

"Wow, this is cool! I don't ever remember seeing this here before," Savannah said. Penny ran to the spring for a drink, but stopped short and barked at the moving water. She sniffed all around it and finally lapped up a healthy drink. Savannah wondered if last night's happenings had opened a fissure, somehow allowing this spring to come alive.

They finished riding the back half of the farm. Seeing nothing unusual, they headed back to GiGi's house. As they rode together down the trail with Penny racing ahead, Savannah volunteered that GiGi had been very upset lately, but especially last night, when she had confided to Savannah that if something were to happen to her, she needed Savannah to be strong for her mom. Then this morning, Savannah had noticed GiGi's red eyes and thought she had been crying. Savannah said she had tried to comfort GiGi but didn't really know how. Maybe her mom would have some answers when she got home from work.

They stopped by the new spring and both of them were thinking the same thing: *Why not stop and take a look around?* "Maybe there's a lake for swimming...just kidding," laughed Savannah. "Let's just see where it's coming from."

They left their bikes on the trail and wandered back about three-quarters of a mile along the spring. Penny started barking again. "What is it, girl?" asked Savannah.

"Maybe it's a rabbit," suggested Michael Henry. "Let's take a look." Penny approached an opening in the rock. She darted in. As they followed Penny's lead, Michael Henry thought about his vision from last night. What did it really mean?

When they entered the small opening, they could smell a very old, musty odor. "This smell reminds me of opening up our underground storage cellar after the snow melts in the early spring. Very earthen, yet very different indeed."

Michael Henry got out his flashlight and shone it on the walls around the cavern in front of him. The LED light illuminated the glasslike surroundings. As she looked around, Savannah exclaimed, "This cavern is all crystal!" She reached out, taking Michael Henry's outstretched hand, and pointed it to a large stalactite. The flashlight immediately illuminated this piece, giving off a low-level light. As Michael Henry changed his hand position, he was able to illuminate ten more structures, both stalactites and stalagmites, for a warm, eerie, low level of light throughout the cavern.

He squeezed Savannah's hand. "I need to tell you something."

"What is it?"

"Well, for the last two nights I've had weird dreams, saying that I am the Chosen One for our time, and that the Medallion will be in contact with me. It also said that you would lead me to an entrance where I would find a portal that I'm supposed to illuminate with my flashlight. Pretty strange, huh?"

Savannah looked at him with amazement and said she'd known there was something different about him, but hadn't known exactly what it was. They walked straight ahead and he briefly pointed his flashlight towards the round, glasslike structures. These clear, resplendent mounds lit up with strange names in green lights embedded in the smooth crystal. Michael Henry shone the flashlight on one such area only to have it light up as if there were lightning going

9

through it. It was a bright white light with green letters: "The Land of Whoo."

Michael Henry remembered his instructions from his dream the night before. He mumbled the words under his breath as Savannah looked on in amazement. "Shine your light once and this will illuminate the portal."

Then in a low, deep, resonating voice, the portal demanded, "Who are you?"

His reply came quickly. "Michael Henry, the Chosen One, and Savannah James." As he spoke, another round of exquisite white and green flashes were joined by rays that extended in all directions and included all the colors of the rainbow. The portal immediately opened. Its words were very clear: "You are free to enter." They were whisked away to a clearing with buttercups and fields of waving green grass.

The messenger appeared to Michael Henry and Savannah as they arrived. "Welcome, Michael Henry, the Chosen One. We have been expecting you for some time. Follow the path to the castle on the hill, where you will be given further instructions. You are free to leave and return to the Land of Whoo as you wish, but you must tell no one of your mission or the location of the Whoo Portal. Great powers await you."

"What powers?"

"The power of health over illness, the power of strength over weakness, the power of light over darkness. But the power of the Chosen One is to be used wisely, with no malice toward any person or creature. The people and the creatures in the Land of Whoo welcome you both."

Savannah was trembling. "I want to go back! This is just too much for me right now!"

Michael Henry could sense her weakness, and they turned around and hurried down the path and back through the portal. Penny was still in the cavern, wagging her tail and ever so glad to see them. As they walked away, the portal said in a low, husky voice, "Tell no one—lives are at stake." The portal went dark as they walked slowly out of the cavern.

Michael Henry looked first towards the opening and then at Savannah. Their thoughts were the same: *What just happened?* They were both trying to understand. Neither spoke as they covered the entrance to the cavern with some brush that was lying on the ground by the opening. They walked silently to their bikes. Then Michael Henry almost exploded. "Wow, what was *that*? We've had a busy day!"

Just then he got a text from his dad: "We're going out tonight for a family night because we've all been working so hard since we moved in. Also to celebrate—Mom got a promotion and a raise! Be home by 6 tonight, son. Love u, Dad."

Savannah was still shaking. "I'm scared, Michael Henry. What should we do?"

"For now, tell no one of our trip today. Let's head back. I have to go home too. My mom got a promotion at work and we're going out."

"That's great!" They rode back down the cattle trail to the main road, where they said goodbye. Michael Henry rode toward his house, thoughts swirling in his head, while Savannah headed back to the farmhouse.

GiGi greeted her with a big hug. "How was your day, honey?"

Savannah was glad to be home and felt safe as she hugged her grandmother back. "It looks like there was no damage from the small quake last night, GiGi."

They walked arm in arm to the kitchen. GiGi poured herself a cup of Starbucks Breakfast Blend and added some cream and sugar. "Sit down, Savannah. We need to talk for a minute before your mom gets home from work." Savannah walked over to the kitchen table and sat down. "Savannah," began GiGi, "I haven't been feeling well lately and have had numerous tests done. Your mom accompanied me for all of them. It appears that I have a rare and fatal disease called CJD, or Creutzfeldt-Jakob disease. We've been contacting major clinics around the country to check on advanced treatments. During my appointment today, Dr. Clark told me to enjoy life as long as I could. If I take the regimen of expensive medicines he is prescribing, he estimates I have less than a year to live. Honey, we are trying to see what insurance will pay for. I told your mom I wanted to tell you, and she wanted to go find Paul and tell him."

Savannah cried as she heard the news. Her GiGi was dying. What could she do? "GiGi, there must be something the doctors can do," she said through her tears.

"Honey, we have already exhausted all of our avenues. All I want is to enjoy the time I have left with you and your mother."

CHAPTER 2

MICHAEL HENRY FINDS HIS ANCESTRY

Savannah woke to the sounds of GiGi crying with her daughter. "I told Savannah the news that I was not long for this world. She is more mature than I could have known. I will surely miss both of you—I really wanted to see her grow up. I've been thinking of selling the farm and using the money to take you and Savannah on a long trip before the inevitable happens, but then I think of how much you and Savannah love this farm where you were raised and realize that I want to keep it in the family."

Leslie said she would not know how to act without her mother and best friend. They embraced, and Savannah let them cry for a long time before she dared to walk into the room.

"Well, good morning, Sunshine. How's my girl this morning?" Leslie asked, wiping the tears from her eyes. "GiGi told me there's a new man in your life."

Savannah blushed. "Yeah, he's new at the Academy and has dropped by on his bike a couple of times. No big deal, Mom. What about you and GiGi?" she asked, conveniently changing the subject.

"Oh, honey," said GiGi, "we never meant to leave you out of anything. Let's enjoy the time we have together. Today your mom and I have an appointment with an attorney to review my final wishes."

Savannah hugged her grandmother. "GiGi, don't worry about me. I'll be fine. And Mom's new friend, Paul, seems to be getting more serious, so…" Her voice trailed off as she looked at her mom. Leslie smiled and remained quiet. "You and Mom take care of whatever you need to do, GiGi. I still have faith that a miracle will happen if we let it."

"Okay, Savannah," said GiGi, her beautiful smile returning to her face. "I can't argue with that! I'm very impressed with your positive attitude, but it's also time to be realistic. Everything known to modern medicine gives me less than one year to live, but let's not be concerned with that today. You take Penny and check on the animals, and we'll be back later so we can all have dinner together. Maybe that new guy will drop by again."

The three walked to the kitchen and made breakfast together. They sat down to a delicious meal of scrambled eggs with cheese, just the way Savannah liked them, and toast with GiGi's homemade strawberry jelly. It made Savannah remember how much fun they'd had the year before at the Strawberry Festival, and she wondered if GiGi would be there for the festivities next year. She cleared the dishes while her mom and GiGi headed out the door for their appointment with the attorney in downtown Seattle.

Savannah felt a vibration and checked her phone. It was a text from Michael Henry. "Would like to venture to Whoo. Can we go together???"

Savannah texted back, "Absolutely. I have more reasons now to go with u."

Michael Henry's reply came quickly, "Be at the gate in 30 minutes."

Savannah hit "K" and sent the text. She just had a couple of things to finish up before she was ready to leave.

Michael Henry was almost bubbly about the prospect of going back to the hidden cavern and the portal. The two friends rode right to the site after leaving Penny at the farm. Once they arrived, they noticed the brush had been forcibly moved from the entrance. There were three-foot-long, eagle-like feathers on the ground and tracks all around the opening leading to the cavern. Michael Henry wondered what had been there.

As if reading his mind, Savannah pointed to the imprints. "Some wild bird must have been caught in the brush." What they did not know was that a creature from the Land of Whoo had come through the portal that morning, sent by the Dark Wizard, on a mission to destroy Michael Henry.

Michael Henry took his trusty LED flashlight and illuminated the cavern, just as he had done the day before. He walked directly to the Whoo Portal and shone his light in the center. Like yesterday, after his identity was verified, it lit up with all the colors of the rainbow. The pair walked briskly through the portal. Once in the Land of Whoo, Michael Henry turned to Savannah and asked, "Why the sudden change of heart? Yesterday you couldn't wait to get out of here!"

"My grandmother GiGi is very sick with a fatal disease. Her only chance is for a miracle. I'm hoping you *are* the Chosen One to save her and that we will find the answer here."

"Wow, that sounds pretty serious, Savannah. I may not be up for that much responsibility."

Savannah looked at her new friend. "Not to worry, Michael Henry. I have a good feeling about you and this Land of Whoo."

No sooner had the words come out of her mouth than they saw a man on a large wagon being pulled by two horse-like creatures, barreling towards them as fast as they could go. The driver yelled to them as he approached, "You are in danger! Hop on board so I can get you to safety!"

The portal behind them closed with a whir. Michael Henry and Savannah jumped in the wagon, and the man in the brown robe threw a tarp over them. They raced away as fast as they had arrived.

"Where are we going?" Michael Henry shouted over the noise of the wagon.

The man in the robe turned his head to be sure they weren't being followed. "My name is Clive, and I have instructions to deliver you safely to the castle to meet the king and queen of Whoo. We have been expecting you, Michael Henry. You are the Chosen One and we must be careful!"

"Why all the secrecy, Clive?"

His eyes still scanning the horizon, Clive answered, "The Dark Wizard knows of your existence and has sent his creatures to look for you. He has foreseen your strength and wants to destroy you for his own safety and the safety of his commander, Master Uror."

As they rode away from the portal, Savannah wondered what she had gotten herself into. But she remained hopeful, since she trusted Michael Henry.

"We will be stopping soon," continued Clive, "to change carriers and give you a break." They pulled up to an inn with a large compass on top and the name Four Corners underneath. Clive hustled them inside. He handed each of them a change of clothes so they wouldn't stand out from the locals. They both went to change while Clive ordered drinks and food for them all. When they returned, he showed them to their seats just as plates of charbroiled meat and potatoes were being placed on the round table, along with bread and a bowl of what tasted like clam chowder. The three sat down to eat their meal. It wasn't McDonald's, but it sure tasted good! The visitors had one question after another for their driver, but all Clive would say was that Michael Henry was the

Chosen One and that his mission was to deliver Michael Henry and Savannah to the Castle of New Providence to meet with the king and queen.

"What are they like?" asked Savannah. "The king and queen, that is."

Clive didn't divulge much information, saying only that they would see soon enough. He did tell them that the king had lost his son in the war with the Dark Wizard and the warlord Master Uror.

As soon as they were done eating, they climbed back in the wagon and were off, racing once again down the dusty road towards the Castle. As they neared their destination, they saw crowds lining the streets. Word had traveled far and wide that the king of Whoo was coming out to address his people about the state of the war.

As the king stepped out onto his balcony to begin his speech, Michael Henry and Savannah were rushed into the castle through a secret passage so no one would be aware of their arrival. Clive arranged for a change of clothes and servants led them down separate hallways, each ending in a large room with pools of warm, sparkly water. They certainly needed to wash off the layers of dust they had collected on the wagon ride to the castle. As Michael Henry finished dressing, Clive came in and said that King Titus was ready to meet with him as soon as he was ready. Savannah was brushing her hair when Queen Coreen's handmaiden, Jasmine, arrived to tell her that the queen would like to see her when she was ready. Michael Henry and Savannah were then taken to the royal quarters to finally meet King Titus and Queen Coreen.

King Titus greeted Michael Henry with a kiss on each cheek and presented him with a gold ring for his finger. There appeared to be a coin in the middle of the striking piece of jewelry. "Michael Henry, I am King Titus."

Surprised, Michael Henry asked, "How do you know of me, and how do you know my name?"

King Titus looked at him with an expression that made Michael Henry feel at home. "You are indeed the Chosen One, and your arrival has been foretold for many, many years. Let me explain it from the beginning. The Land of Whoo had always been a very peaceful place. Then the Dark Wizard and Master Uror combined their powers to attack the kingdom at the first Castle of Providence, our original home, outside of the Crystal City. Many of my people perished while defending the kingdom, and we were eventually driven away to our current home here at New Providence after years of fighting. The Dark Wizard and Master Uror, after taking our lands and our castle, enslaved many of our people to serve them in the fertile lands of Providence. We were left with this rocky and barren portion of Whoo.

"Eventually we found that we were sitting on vast deposits of powerful crystals, and we discovered the portal that allowed you and Savannah to travel to our land. Years went by and an envoy was sent through the portal to Earth. That envoy, Michael Henry, was led by your mother, Princess Marie, who was carrying you. We were not aware of it at the time, but we later understood that you would be the Chosen One for our time.

"Princess Marie was the daughter of my closest friend and ally, Count Aiden. She and my son, Prince Knox, were married prior to the outbreak of the Great War. She was very beautiful and very cunning. She had mastered the power of the Medallion and used its power instinctively to free many of our oppressed citizens. The tide of the war was turning in our favor, due in part to Knox's charisma and leadership.

"The Dark Wizard and Master Uror sensed this change in power as their attacks became more devastating. The Dark Wizard was charged with a secret operation to lure your father into a trap, along with many brave soldiers. As you know, the Medallion has the power of health over illness. When my son was struck down, Princess Marie could have saved him using the power of the Medallion, except that the Dark Wizard had used a very strong, fast-acting poisonous gas. Your mother sensed your father's dire situation as he lay wounded and immediately rushed to his side. Unfortunately, it was too late.

"Your mother was heartbroken and distressed beyond belief as she realized she was unable to save him. There was nothing she could do except kiss him goodbye for the last time. Princess Marie sensed that in her current state, she would be an easy target for the Dark Wizard and Master Uror. She knew that they would certainly plan some way to take control of the Medallion, putting its tremendous powers to work against our people, so she did the unthinkable and sacrificed herself for the good of her people. She enshrined the Medallion under the care of your uncle Jonathon, who would also sacrifice life as he knew it to be the messenger for the Medallion. He waited for Princess Marie's return when conditions in the Land of Whoo stabilized.

"Michael Henry, your mother traveled through the portal to Earth without the power of the Medallion; however, she was able to communicate by thought with Jonathon and the Medallion. She let them know that she was with child, that the child's name would be Michael Henry, and that when the time was right, he would return to the Land of Whoo. In the meantime, the portal would be completely safe, since the Medallion's signature was masked completely because it was hidden in the Crystal City.

"The last message we received from Princess Marie was that she had sealed the portal completely so no one would be allowed passage and the Dark Wizard would not be able to track her in any way. The Medallion has the power to communicate with you through the messenger, your uncle Jonathon. After you have found its hidden location, there will be five trials, just like there had been for your mother, Princess Marie, allowing the Medallion to verify that you are, indeed, the Chosen One.

19

"We have a kept guard posted at the portal all these years, waiting for your arrival. There were also markers installed by the Dark Wizard. Once the portal opened, he became aware of your existence and sent a condor through to search for and destroy you. You must now go back through the portal, being careful to close and seal it properly. The portal will ask who you are. Answer, 'I am Michael Henry, the Chosen One. I wish to return. Let no man or creature travel through this portal until my return.'

"Then, using these poisonous crystals, you must destroy the condor. These condors have a reputation of not returning to their masters, so all will be forgotten soon. Once this is accomplished, the messenger will contact you."

King Titus then led Michael Henry to the royal quarters, where Savannah and Queen Coreen had been talking. They sat down together for dinner. After the main course was served, King Titus said, "Michael Henry, you will need to return through the portal tonight. Tell no one of our conversation. When you return, bring Savannah with you. She has your best interests at heart."

They finished their meal, and then Michael Henry followed the instructions given him by his grandfather, King Titus.

CHAPTER 3

ATTACK OF THE CONDOR

Michael Henry and Savannah departed through the portal, their clothes changing back to the same jeans and T-shirts they had been wearing before they arrived in the Land of Whoo. As they were leaving the cavern and covering the entrance, a large, squawking creature dive-bombed the pair. It had to be the condor they had been warned about! They ran to their bikes and pedaled as fast as their legs would allow, given the rough cattle trail.

The condor dove again and again, trying to knock them off their bikes. The area was thick with large trees, making it hard for the bird to zero in on its prey. Michael Henry and Savannah headed for the farmhouse. He remembered a pond on the edge of the large field near the house. As they peddled down the road, he recalled the hundred-pound fishing line GiGi had strung above the pond to keep the birds from diving on her koi in the pond. "Savannah, let's head for the small gazebo by the pond!" he shouted as the condor dove at them.

They finally made it to the pond by the gazebo, and the condor dove again at its target. There was little light left to reflect on the monofilament lines. As the pair approached the gazebo, Penny came bounding towards them from the farmhouse to help with the fight, barking excitedly at the huge bird. The distracted condor became entangled in a dozen of the lines and fell to the ground adjacent to the pond.

Michael Henry pounced on him before the condor knew what had hit it. He thrust one of the poisonous crystals into the condor, then the other. He noticed that the condor's feet were like eagle talons that could pick up prey as he dove. "Quick, Savannah, bring the tiki fuel and lighter from the gazebo!" Soon, what was left of the condor was burnt and then quietly buried. The pair headed for the farmhouse and waited to see if any other creatures were about. They leaned their bikes against the steps to the porch. Speculating that the crystals may be useful in the future, Michael Henry placed them carefully into his backpack.

They looked around and realized no one was home yet. Savannah was relieved, trying to imagine how she would have explained the condor.

"So, Savannah, what happened to you while we were separated at the castle?"

"Oh, Michael Henry, Queen Coreen took me into her confidence and told me a bit of the history of the Land of Whoo."

"What did she tell you?"

"Well, it seems the Land of Whoo was a quiet, peaceful place before the war. Then the Dark Wizard and warlord Master Uror combined forces to split the kingdom. There was a huge battle, and the king and queen's son, Prince Knox, was killed. His wife, Princess Marie, had the tremendous power of something called the Medallion but couldn't reach her husband in time to save his life. She was so distraught, she hid the Medallion and followed the king's instructions to leave through the portal to be safe and, once on the other side, seal the portal."

Michael Henry glanced down sadly. "I know. That was my birth mother and father. What else did she tell you?"

"She told me that the Dark Wizard has a number of creatures at his disposal."

"Like what?"

"There are majors, creepy, bright red crabs that are as big as the royal carriage when they become adults. They are sent against an enemy with their two-foot-long claws that can crush a tree or a human limb. Then there are minors. These are the juvenile crabs that are very fast and can outrun a human in a fifty-yard race. They are light gray and can be camouflaged very easily.

"There are also creatures called ten-eyes, whose ten eyes are at the end of long tubes, like snakes, coming from their slimy brown bodies. The adults are usually six to seven feet long and can strangle an enemy that comes too close. The juvenile ten-eyes are bright green and can move even faster than the adults."

Just then they saw a car coming up the driveway, and they went out to meet Savannah's mom and GiGi.

"Well, this must be Michael Henry," said Leslie with a smile as they neared the car.

"A pleasure to meet you, ma'am," said Michael Henry as he shook hands with both Leslie and GiGi. "Well, it's getting late and I need to get home. Nice to meet you," he said as he rode off.

Wow, what a day, he thought as he passed the gate to the farmhouse. He made it home just as his mom and dad were pulling in the driveway.

"Anything special happen today, Michael Henry?" asked his mom as she got out of the car.

"Yes, I went to Savannah's farm, and we explored part of the countryside," Michael Henry answered as he leaned his bike against the porch.

"Sounds great."

They watched a bit of TV together after dinner and then went to bed. That night, Michael Henry was again visited in a dream by the messenger of the Medallion,

Jonathon. "Michael Henry, now you have evidence that you are the Chosen One. The secrets and awesome power of the Medallion await. We have discovered that the Dark Wizard is preparing another attack on the Castle of New Providence to destroy King Titus and Queen Coreen. He has heard the prophecy that you will be returning to use the powers of the Medallion against his forces in the near future. The Dark Wizard and Master Uror have spies everywhere, watching. Your people need you, Your Majesty. Do not delay your return to the Land of Whoo."

CHAPTER 4

TRAVEL TO THE STAR PORTAL

Michael Henry lay in bed the next morning with questions swirling in his head. What preparations should he make before returning to Whoo? What was the strange feeling of confidence that had come over him once he emerged from the portal and set foot in the Land of Whoo? Was he really the Chosen One? Would he be able to save GiGi? Was he really capable of finding the Medallion and unlocking its amazing secrets as his birth mother had done? And what had happened to his mother, Princess Marie? What was she like? He somehow knew the answers would be revealed in time, but for now, first things first: How should he prepare for his mission?

He had a medium-sized backpack and started thinking about what to take with him. The crystals were already at the bottom, but what should he add? Of course he needed his LED flashlight with extra batteries to open the portal. He remembered the pair of walkie-talkies he had received last Christmas. They could possibly help him maintain contact if he and Savannah should become separated, as they had on the last trip. He would also bring a lighter and a package of six rockets he had left over from last year's Fourth of July celebration with his family. He closed the zipper and headed downstairs for some breakfast.

At the farmhouse, Savannah got out of bed. A week had passed since their last trip to the Land of Whoo. She could hear voices through the air vent that ran from her room to the kitchen and wondered what her mom and GiGi were talking about. It sounded like they were discussing one last hope above all hopes. GiGi's doctor, Dr. Clark, had set up an appointment with a world-renowned specialist, a Dr. Jordan, who also happened to be a friend of Dr. Clark's from medical school. Evidently Dr. Jordan had come to Seattle to further his research at the university hospital. He was recognized worldwide for his straightforward attitude and had agreed to review GiGi's records and do an examination. Once they met with Dr. Jordan, he would order any additional tests he thought were necessary. He would then hopefully be able to put together all of GiGi's information and come up with the answers they wanted by the end of the week.

The door to Savannah's room opened slowly as Leslie looked in to see if her daughter was awake. "Good morning, Savannah. GiGi and I are going in to Seattle to see a new specialist, Dr. Jordan. He's agreed to review her history and give us his opinion as to what our options really are. We're leaving shortly. Will you be okay for a few hours here at the farm, or do you want to go with us?"

Savannah was torn between wanting to be with GiGi and staying at the farm. She thought again about what the messenger had told Michael Henry—the power of health over illness. Convinced she could help more by returning to the Land of Whoo with the Chosen One, Savannah hugged her mom and said, "I'll be okay here. Good luck."

As her mom walked down the hall to finish getting ready, Savannah texted Michael Henry. "Mom and GiGi are going to Seattle today for more tests. I want to go back to the Land of Whoo to search for a cure for GiGi."

26

Michael Henry felt the vibration, looked at his phone, and responded, "I agree, let's return to Whoo. See you soon." He grabbed his backpack and was off to Savannah's. He arrived just as GiGi and Leslie were turning onto the main road. They waved as they passed and he waved back. When he got to the farmhouse, he noticed Savannah had her bike ready to go. They both jumped on their bikes and headed down the main road to the cattle trail towards the entrance to the cavern. When they arrived, it appeared that no one had discovered the opening. After they cleared the brush aside, the pair entered the cavern. Michael Henry shone his flashlight on the stalagmites and stalactites, illuminating the chamber with a low-level light as he and Savannah approached the portal.

"Stand back, Savannah," he said, and pointed the flashlight towards the portal inscribed "The Land of Whoo."

The portal immediately shone brighter and demanded, "Who are you?"

"I am Michael Henry, the Chosen One, and I need to change the portal settings now."

The portal opened for their passage. "How may I assist you?" it asked.

"Who knows of my travel through this portal?"

"The Dark Wizard has directed that a notification be sent to him if anyone uses it."

"Portal, from now on, I want his command cancelled, and I want you to be protected against unauthorized entry. Send no further notifications to anyone. Is that clear?"

"Yes, Master," the portal responded.

"I also want you to take a very close look at my eyes. Do not allow entrance to anyone or anything that does not have my exact eye configuration, especially my pupils. Can you do this?"

"Yes, Master," said the portal, sending out a light beam to measure and record Michael Henry's pupils.

Michael Henry thought for a moment. "How many portals are there in the Land of Whoo?"

"From this portal, you have access to three - the one you traveled through on your first journey to Whoo, and two others."

"Where are the other two?"

"One was known only by your mother. It is called the Star Portal because of its shape and is located high on a mountain peak above the Castle of New Providence. The other is near the old Castle of Providence. It is also known to the Dark Wizard and is called the Dark Portal, so named by your mother because of its close proximity to the Dark Wizard's castle. There is a sled at the Star Portal that can be instructed to provide transportation. There is a landing pad atop the Castle of New Providence, or you may land the sled on King Titus' private balcony. You are able to have the sled deliver you anywhere of your choosing."

"Portal, do you connect to the other two portals and will my commands be communicated to them, or do I need to instruct them separately?"

"Master, whatever you convey to one portal is understood and complied with by all."

"Portal, reset and communicate my commands now to the other portals." With Michael Henry's words, the portal immediately turned back to a blank crystal, the words "The Land of Whoo" now encased deep inside.

Once the portal had closed, Michael Henry shone his flashlight into it again. "Who are you?" asked the portal.

"I am Michael Henry, the Chosen One."

The portal advised him to place his head in a small crevice next to the large crystal. Immediately a light illuminated his face and scanned his eyes for verification, just as he had requested. When the scan was complete, the portal opened, and Michael Henry said, "Take me to the Star Portal in the Land of Whoo."

He and Savannah walked into the portal and were transported to a cavern in the Land of Whoo. It looked very familiar, just like the first portal, but it was very, very cold. There was a rack of parkas in different sizes alongside the opening. They each chose a jacket that would fit and hoped it would keep out the cold. Michael Henry looked around and shone his flashlight on the stalagmites and stalactites, illuminating them each in turn. In the middle of this area was a crystal pedestal with a bright yellow crystal in the middle of it. He remembered that King Titus had mentioned that his mother's favorite color was yellow. Slowly he approached the pedestal and removed the yellow crystal. Immediately a hologram of Princess Marie appeared.

"Who are you?" the image asked.

"Michael Henry, the Chosen One, and Savannah James, my friend from Earth."

Princess Marie started crying. "My son, I have hoped beyond hope you would find this cavern and the secret Star Portal! My prayers have been answered—you are still safe after all these years. And look how you have grown!"

"Mother, what am I to do?"

"Michael Henry, do not be afraid. The Medallion will be with you soon to protect you and Savannah from harm. First you must take the sled to the Inn of Ethan. Once there, ask the sled to fly to the Castle of New Providence and bring King Titus to you, telling no one of your return to the Land of Whoo. Second, you must seek shelter. Tell the innkeeper you need a room for the night, and you want the Princess Marie Room. The rooms are named after the royal family. Inside the parkas you are wearing is a hidden pouch with enough money to give the innkeeper for your stay. Go in alone and have Savannah follow you later, after you are settled. Savannah should stay in the sled, since it will be invisible to all others.

"Third, once in the room, there will be a locked door. There is a sign on the door that says 'Entrance to the Prince

Knox Room,' which is the room next door. Use the key in your parka to open this door. As it opens, it will ask you, 'Who are you?' You will need to reply, 'Michael Henry, the Chosen One.' It will lead to a workshop below the inn that has been sealed since I left. Once inside, you will see where your father worked on his weapons and armor. King Titus will need to send you the two skilled craftsmen who helped your father. If they have passed away, their sons will be familiar with all that your father was working on. Use the knowledge you have inherited from me to devise a plan to enter the Crystal City. Once inside its borders, the Medallion will seek you out.

"Tell no one of your plans, not even King Titus, as he may have traitors in his ranks. I love you, my son."

As Michael Henry replaced the yellow crystal, their time together ended. He turned to Savannah, his eyes opened wide. They both buttoned up the warm coats. He and Savannah, wearing their heavy parkas and the gloves they found in the pockets, left the protection of the cavern. They saw three sleds parked near the entrance in the snow. Each was about ten feet long, with a seat in the rear and two wooden handles in the front with which to steer, just like the sleds back home.

In the rear seat were two pairs of goggles, which they placed on their heads and pulled down over their eyes, hoping for some protection from the heavy snow falling from the dark skies. Michael Henry laid down to drive, and Savannah sat down quickly in the rear seat. As soon as he touched the handles, the sled seemed to come alive.

"Who are you?" it demanded.

Michael Henry answered as he had so many times before, "Michael Henry, the Chosen One."

The sled responded, "Welcome, Master. What is your command?"

"First I want to fly this sled by myself to see how it feels. Once I am familiar with how you handle, I want you to take us to the Inn of Ethan. What shall I call you?"

"Master, your mother was the last one to give me instructions, and she called me her Cuatro Star, as my home is this secret Star Portal. She credits me with saving her life four times before she fully discovered how to use the Medallion."

Michael Henry wondered what dangers his mother had survived. "Okay, Cuatro Star, how do I operate the sled?"

"Master, you can give me a verbal command like your mother did, or if you wish, you can control me by hand, like your father did. Push the handle forward for more speed. Pull the handle up to rise, and down to dive. Also, Master, when you are driving, it would be a good idea to use the ties on the seat next to you to secure yourself on the sled to keep from falling off."

Michael Henry looked back over his shoulder at Savannah and told her to tie herself in. This was going to be amazing! He took off straight up and did a loop-the-loop, ending with a sharp dive. He pulled the handle up to bring the sled out of the spiral and followed the snowy valley, only to rise again to the mountaintops. What great fun! Savannah yelled that she was feeling sick, and he straightened out the sled. He commanded Cuatro to take them slowly to the Inn of Ethan and to remain invisible unless otherwise instructed.

Once they landed, Michael Henry walked in as if he owned the place. He walked right up to the innkeeper and said, "I need a room, please, and quickly. I wish to have the Princess Marie Room."

The innkeeper said his name was Ethan, and that business had been very slow lately. Taking note of Michael Henry's age, he asked, "How are you planning to pay for the room?"

Michael Henry tossed five gold coins from his pocket on the counter. He told Ethan that he did not wish to be disturbed. Ethan gave him the key and asked if he needed anything else. Realizing they hadn't eaten since breakfast, he asked the innkeeper to make him a large lunch of roasted chicken and leave it outside his door.

"Yes, Master," Ethan said. "May I help you unload your coach outside?"

"That will not be necessary, Ethan. I am travelling very light and wish you to prepare my lunch, please."

After Michael Henry was settled in his room, he went to Cuatro to get Savannah. She hopped off the sled, and Michael Henry told Cuatro to go to the Castle of New Providence and bring King Titus. He and Savannah entered the inn together and headed straight for the stairway leading to his room. Once they were both inside, he showed Savannah the door with the sign that read "Entrance to the Prince Knox Room." He opened it using the key in his parka, and the two friends walked down the stairway to his father's workshop.

Inside the large room were two pedestals resembling the one in the Star Portal cavern. There was a yellow crystal in one and a blue crystal in the other. Michael Henry lifted the yellow crystal up out of its holder and a hologram of his mother appeared once again. "Michael Henry, you are safe here. You have finally discovered this workshop, so now, your father, Prince Knox, has a message for you. I, too, have many things to tell you, but first lift up the blue crystal so you will understand what your father needs you to do."

With his hand trembling, Michael Henry lifted the larger blue crystal out of its receptacle. Prince Knox appeared immediately. "My son, I see you have finally come. As you must know by now, I perished in the battle against the Dark Wizard and Master Uror. Once they learn of your existence in the Land of Whoo, they will attempt to kill you as well. Do not be afraid. You were sent here for a reason, and the

Medallion has grown more powerful since it was last used by your beloved mother.

"First of all, welcome. The Inn of Ethan has been in our family for many generations, and the innkeeper and his family have all sworn their allegiance to us. However, there is no reason to put them in jeopardy by revealing any of your plans to them. As we once found out, they will be tortured by the Dark Wizard. You must act quickly, my son. Have my father, King Titus, bring you my two skilled craftsmen to make you a suit of the same lightweight armor I once had. They must fashion you a sword also. They will make anything else you desire if you only give them specific instructions to do so. Contact your mother and myself as often as you feel necessary. Remember, do not be afraid. You inherited the vast powers your mother once possessed, and my determination."

There was a knock on the outside door. Michael Henry placed the crystal back in its holder and ran up the stairs. Through the peephole he could see a tray of roasted chicken, bread, and a purple beverage in a pitcher. As he opened the door, he saw King Titus walking at a brisk pace toward his room, a cloak around his shoulders and head. As he entered, they brought in the tray, and the trio all hugged and started on their lunch.

Michael Henry shared his adventures since he had last seen King Titus and invited him down to the workshop. Once inside, he removed the blue crystal and his father appeared. King Titus broke down sobbing as he saw his son's image in front of him.

"Do not be afraid," Prince Knox said. "Ask any questions you may have."

"How do we know what the Dark Wizard is up to, and how do we avoid his coming attack?" Michael Henry asked.

"Great questions, my son. Please look on my workshop bench, and you will see a yo-yo. I was working on it before I left and did not have a chance to test it. This yo-yo has an eyeball on the side of it. Drop the yo-yo, and as it reaches the end of the line, give it a hard yank, breaking the string. Command it to change its shape and multiply, becoming dragonflies. These dragonflies will be about three inches long, just like other dragonflies throughout our countryside. Instruct the yo-yo to have the dragonflies bring you information concerning the Dark Wizard and Master Uror. Command the eye to have these dragonflies report back in twenty-four hours. The eye will assimilate this information and find your sled. The sled will then bring the eye to you."

"Very well," answered Michael Henry. He walked to the workshop bench and returned with the yo-yo.

As he used it, the eye came alive and asked, "What are your wishes?"

"I am Michael Henry, the Chosen One. I command you to multiply and change shape into one hundred dragonflies. Have all of the dragonflies return to you after twenty-four hours. You will then return to the invisible sled which will be by the main gate at New Providence Castle, waiting." He yanked the yo-yo's string and broke it just as the eye began changing into dragonflies. Half of the winged creatures headed towards the Dark Wizard and the Castle of Providence, while the other half flew in the direction of Master Uror and the Crystal City.

Michael Henry accompanied his grandfather to Cuatro, and as the king climbed aboard the sled, he assured Michael Henry that the craftsmen were still alive and would be sent right back. Michael Henry pulled the walkie-talkies from his backpack and showed his grandfather how they worked. The king tried his walkie-talkie with disbelief and promised to keep it with him.

King Titus returned within the hour with the same two men Prince Knox had used, along with their sons as apprentices. After the four men stepped off the sled, the king returned to the castle. Michael Henry met them at the door and directed them to the workshop. He instructed them to make two sets of lightweight armor protection and swords. The craftsmen worked into the night while he and Savannah looked on. As they watched the father-and-son teams work, they began to realize how tired they were after such a full day. The two friends sat down on a bench and soon fell asleep, not waking until the next morning to the pounding of the craftsmen working on the finishing touches for their suits of armor and swords.

CHAPTER 5

CAPTURED BY THE DARK WIZARD

Jasmine, the handmaiden of Queen Coreen, went to her room and dispatched a carrier pigeon to the Dark Wizard with the following message: "Michael Henry has returned today to the Land of Whoo."

Queen Coreen had entrusted her handmaiden with this most secret information, even though her husband had told her to tell no one of Michael Henry's return. She was unaware that Jasmine's parents had been kidnapped and were being held hostage in the Dark Wizard's dungeons. He had threatened them with torture and inevitable death if Jasmine did not cooperate.

Within a few hours, the carrier pigeon returned with a reply from the Dark Wizard. "Jasmine," the note said, "your mother and father will be tortured at daybreak and executed at noon if I do not receive the exact location of Michael Henry, the Chosen One."

Jasmine hastily returned to Queen Coreen, thinking only of her parents' safety. She paid close attention to any conversations about Michael Henry. "I hope Michael Henry has found a safe hiding place," she said finally. "Is he in the castle? I would like to see Savannah James again, if she came with him."

Queen Coreen, not even realizing the information she was supplying, replied, "Yes, Jasmine, Michael Henry and Savannah James are safe at the Inn of Ethan, and we expect to see them soon."

"That is great news, Your Majesty. I look forward to their arrival as well."

Queen Coreen excused her handmaiden, and Jasmine hurried back to her room. She went to the window and released the carrier pigeon back to the Dark Wizard with the following message attached to its leg: "Michael Henry is at the Inn of Ethan but will be leaving soon. Now release my parents. I have paid your price."

Meanwhile, Michael Henry was anxiously waiting at the Inn of Ethan for the return of his sled from outside the Castle of New Providence, knowing the information gathered by the one hundred dragonflies would be crucial in determining his next steps. The yo-yo had gathered secret information on the Dark Wizard and Master Uror's activities and reported the following: "Michael Henry, you are in grave danger. The Dark Wizard was seen receiving a message from Jasmine, Queen Coreen's handmaiden, who revealed your location here at the Inn of Ethan. Jasmine's parents were kidnapped and are being held hostage in the Dark Wizard's dungeon. Also, Master Uror is planning an attack on the Castle of New Providence soon. Even now his soldiers are preparing for the battle. He has offered a reward for the heads of King Titus – and you!"

Michael Henry crossed the room to the pedestals. He removed the yellow crystal from its holder. As the hologram appeared, he said, "Mother, this is Michael Henry. The Dark Wizard is sending his troops here to capture me. What should I do?"

"Do not be afraid, Michael Henry. You are the Chosen One. Tell this yellow crystal to multiply into two crystals. Take one with you as you flee from the Inn of Ethan and place the original back in the pedestal. Command the duplicate to become invisible. Then as you leave the workshop, command the crystal to seal the entrance and to open it in the future only for you, and *only* with the duplicate crystal. The Dark Wizard wants you to lead him to the Medallion. Be mindful of this.

"The Medallion is safe in the Crystal City and will direct you on how to approach as you near its location. Once you have freed the Medallion, you will need to pass whatever tests it demands to prove that you are indeed the Chosen One. These tests will be very difficult, but you will prevail as long as the Medallion senses you have no fear and that you are acting for the good of your people and creatures. Remember, you can activate the yellow crystal for my advice at any time. Now you must go, but be advised that the Dark Wizard has many spies. Trust no one, except your immediate friends and family."

Michael Henry grabbed his backpack containing the rockets, flashlight, walkie-talkie, lighter, yellow crystal, and poisonous crystals. He rushed up the stairs with Savannah close behind. The craftsmen were already running down the hallway back to the sled to return to the Castle of New Providence.

As Michael Henry and Savannah reached the top of the stairs, they heard dogs barking loudly in the courtyard. Michael Henry sensed the presence of the Dark Wizard. He sealed the workshop just as the Dark Wizard flew into the room through the open window. Michael Henry grabbed his sword and took a wild swing at the wizard as Savannah ran out of the room towards the stairs. Michael Henry was right behind her, and they bolted down the stairs and out of the inn, trying to escape. The Dark Wizard had stationed a dozen major crabs and another twenty-four minor crabs by the entrance to the Inn of Ethan, along with twenty ten-eyes. Michael Henry sliced the attacking ten-eyes in half with his new sword, but there were just too many. The surviving slimy brown ten-eyes wrapped themselves around Michael Henry.

"Escape to King Titus immediately and await my instructions!" he ordered Cuatro, pushing Savannah onto the sled. "Savannah has dominion over you now." Instantly, the invisible sled was away.

The Dark Wizard smiled. "Unfortunately for you, Michael Henry, I will bring you to my dungeon for torture and execution at sunrise unless you provide me with the Medallion and share its secrets." The ten-eyes immediately tightened their grip and delivered him into the claws of the two giant condors that were waiting to transfer him to the dungeon. One held him by the shoulders and the other grasped his feet as they flew away to the Crystal City, where the Dark Wizard maintained his second command post and dungeons.

As they rose higher and higher, the ten-eyes increased their hold on Michael Henry. He realized he had made a disastrous error in judgment to be captured so easily by the Dark Wizard. In the future he would need to be more prepared and seek additional advice from his mother ahead of time to avoid losing the battle and also have contingency plans in place.

Once they arrived, Michael Henry was immediately placed into a deep, hidden dungeon in the city's tunnel system. Michael Henry's head was spinning from the events, and he speculated on what would happen next. The Dark Wizard commanded the ten-eyes to unravel from Michael Henry as the condors released him. Michael Henry slumped on the ground as the Dark Wizard called for his chief masked torturer to come to the dungeon. He was already on his way and arrived as Michael Henry was trying to assess his situation. The Dark Wizard told the torturer to display his tools and start his fire while Michael Henry mulled over whether he intended to cooperate.

"I will be back within the hour," the wizard said. "I will send a message to the great warlord Master Uror, as he may wish to be present for your torture and execution if you fail to acquiesce and tell me what I want to know."

Back at the Castle of New Providence, Savannah had arrived and commanded the sled to place her on King Titus' outside balcony and await further instructions. The king came out to the balcony when he heard the commotion. He greeted Savannah and then asked where Michael Henry was as the craftsmen exited the sled.

"King Titus, the Dark Wizard surprised us at the Inn of Ethan and captured Michael Henry. Before he was taken, Michael Henry shoved me onto the sled with instructions to come right here. The Dark Wizard's giant condors flew away with Michael Henry in their talons to the Crystal City."

"Oh, Savannah, this is very grave news! Michael Henry is the Chosen One, and with him goes the future of our people and our creatures here in the Land of Whoo. How could the Dark Wizard have known Michael Henry was here in Whoo? The only ones who were aware of his location at the Inn of Ethan were me and the craftsmen."

"King Titus, could you have told anyone else?"

"No, I told no one. Wait—I did mention it to Queen Coreen, but I know she would not have told anyone else."

Sensing the gravity of the situation, Savannah pushed further. "King Titus, the fate of Michael Henry and the Land of Whoo are at stake. Can you please ask her if she knows anything?"

"Very well, my child," he answered and went to find the queen.

A courier brought the message to Master Uror that Michael Henry would be at the Dark Wizard's dungeon. Master Uror was invited to come and await his arrival so he could see the suffering in Michael Henry's face as he was being tortured.

Michael Henry felt the Medallion calling him, saying, "You are near, Michael Henry, in the Crystal City. Proceed to the tower and prepare for your tests."

The Dark Wizard came into Michael Henry's dungeon and gave him the good news. "How exciting! Master Uror wants to come here and witness your torture."

Michael Henry's reply came without hesitation. "Dark Wizard, you have no power over me. I will rain down flames and colored flashes of light over your Crystal City as a warning of things to come, showing that your Master Uror will be destroyed! You should leave now to save yourself from the furor of those held captive in the Crystal City and the Castle of Providence when they are released."

The Dark Wizard laughed a wicked laugh and chided, "I can hardly wait for Master Uror's arrival in my torture chambers. He has imminent plans to attack your pitiful people and creatures at the Castle of New Providence. He is training his soldiers in the city every day and building ramparts for his attack right now, even as we speak, twenty-four hours a day, in the courtyard above the dungeon."

"Your master would not dare attack the Castle at New Providence, knowing that he would surely lose to the forces of King Titus."

"That does it! Bring this insolent creature to the tower so all may hear his screams when Master Uror witnesses the torture with hot knives and hot coals from your fires!" The masked torturer handcuffed Michael Henry and prepared to take him to the tower.

Back at the Castle of New Providence, King Titus asked his wife if, for any reason, she might have told anyone the news that Michael Henry had returned. At first Queen Coreen was very sure of herself and replied, "No, no one, my king." But then, as she thought further, her memory seemed to become more clear. "Oh, wait, I remember now. Yes, I mentioned it to Jasmine yesterday, but we all know she can be trusted."

"Nonetheless, have her brought to me so we can see what she may know," instructed the king.

"Do you really think that is necessary?" She could not imagine that Jasmine could have betrayed them both.

"No, but it will reassure me that we have not inadvertently handed Michael Henry over to the Dark Wizard to be executed. He is our only grandson, and the Chosen One. Time is of the essence."

Jasmine was summoned to the royal quarters. King Titus, Queen Coreen, and Savannah paced back and forth, waiting with bated breath to begin the questioning. After knocking, Jasmine entered the room.

"Jasmine, my dear," the queen said, "it appears that someone in our castle has communicated with the Dark Wizard. As a result of this, my grandson has been captured. Because he is the Chosen One, I am afraid for his life. The only one I spoke to concerning his return was you. Certainly we trust you and know you would not break our confidence, but we must figure out how the Dark Wizard found out where Michael Henry was staying."

Immediately Jasmine broke down. "My queen, I would never do anything to hurt you, but my mother and father have been captured by the Dark Wizard. They were to be tortured at sunrise and put to death at noon unless I revealed Michael Henry's location."

King Titus became very agitated. "Guards! Guards! Take her away to my dungeons for execution tomorrow for treason against the royal family!"

The Dark Wizard had returned to his throne room to relax and freshen up while he waited for his master to arrive. He did wonder about Michael Henry's threats but brushed them aside. He would enjoy seeing Michael Henry suffer at the hands of his masked torturer.

By this time, the torturer had moved Michal Henry to the tower as commanded by the Dark Wizard. All the while Michael Henry yelled, "I will rain down fire on the Crystal

City if you do not release me! Release me now or I will rain down fire upon you! I am Michael Henry, the Chosen One!"

Once Michael Henry was secure in the tower, the torturer returned to the dungeon to pack up his tools and return to the tower for the torture of the Chosen One, as instructed by the Dark Wizard. As he walked, everyone asked about the legends of Michael Henry. Rumors had spread from the Castle of New Providence that the Chosen One was coming to regain the power of the Medallion and save his people and the creatures of Whoo from the Dark Wizard and Master Uror. Was it true? Was he really there?

Michael Henry took out his backpack and was thankful the people of Whoo had no idea what it was. If the Dark Wizard had known what was inside, surely he would have taken it away! Michael Henry pulled out the yellow crystal. "Mother, this is Michael Henry, the Chosen One, and I am being held in the tower by the Dark Wizard in the Crystal City. What should I do to find the Medallion?"

The crystal immediately lit up and a hologram of Princess Marie appeared. "You have done well, my son, to be so close to the Medallion. When you can, ask the yellow crystal to open your tower door and then proceed down the narrow stairs until you come to the second door. Tell the crystal to open this door. By this time, the Medallion will have contacted you."

Just as Michael Henry put the crystal back in his backpack, the masked torturer came back with his wagon. He left it outside of Michael Henry's cell and then entered the small room, lighting a fire in the fire pit. He told Michael Henry that he would be back soon and instructed him to think about what was going to happen when he did return, if he foolishly chose not to cooperate with the Dark Wizard.

As soon as the torturer was out of sight, Michael Henry retrieved the yellow crystal again and, slipping his backpack on, commanded the crystal to open the door, which it did. He proceeded down the stairs. Before he got to the first door, the Medallion contacted him, "You have done well, Michael Henry. Proceed to the second door and open it with the crystal. Illuminate the room. I will be watching you."

Michael Henry opened the second door using the yellow crystal. The door made a creaking noise. No one had opened this door in over a decade. He found himself in a small room with crystal formations coming up from the floor. He shone his flashlight on them. Like the stalactites and stalagmites in the cavern by the portal, they glowed with color reflecting from every shiny surface.

Meanwhile, Savannah had been talking to King Titus and Queen Coreen about Jasmine. She suggested that the maid had only been trying to save her parents and wondered if they should consider using her to give false information to the Dark Wizard after her parents were freed. It could allow them to set a trap for his capture in the future.

"Having lost a son to the Dark Wizard's treachery, I can sympathize with Jasmine. I agree we should give her a chance to redeem herself in the future," said King Titus. "We will discuss it more in the morning and reconsider Jasmine's sentence. Let us all get some rest tonight. We must be ready for whatever tomorrow brings."

Michael Henry was contacted again by the Medallion. A bright light came from the yellow and blue crystal formation in the middle of the room. "Michael Henry, place your hand on the top of this crystal formation and say, 'I am Michael Henry. Let my messenger free.'" Michael Henry did as he was directed, and immediately a tall, muscular man wearing a gold chain with a medallion on it appeared.

"Hello, Michael Henry. I am Jonathon, the Medallion keeper and messenger. I am the one who was in your dreams prior to your finding the portal at the direct request of the all-powerful Medallion. I welcome you back to the Land of Whoo. Are you ready to proceed with your trials for the Medallion?"

"Yes, of course," answered Michael Henry.

"Then let the trials begin." And with Jonathon's words, the door to the room sealed itself shut and the entire chamber began to shake.

CHAPTER 6

LET THE TRIALS BEGIN

Jonathon said, "Are you sure you are ready, Michael Henry? There is no going back once the five trials have begun. Failure to complete any of these trials could expose you to very serious harm—possibly even cause your death."

Michael Henry was ready. "What can I expect after the trials are completed?"

Jonathon answered that after the trials, if the Medallion felt he was worthy, its powers would be completely at his disposal. "Do you remember what I told you in your dream of the powers you will have immediate access to? The power of health over illness, the power of strength over weakness, and the power of light over darkness. The power of the Chosen One is to be used wisely, with no malice toward any person or creature."

"Jonathon, my friend Savannah's grandmother on Earth is suffering from a lethal disease for which there is no known cure. Will the powers I receive from the Medallion enable me to cure her?"

"Of course, as long as you have no malice toward any man or creature on Earth."

"What if the Medallion deems me to be unworthy?"

"I wish you had not asked me that question, Michael Henry. However, since you have, your answer is as follows: the Medallion would disappear from the Land of Whoo and look for another person or creature it deemed worthy. That person would then have to complete the trials in whatever land the Medallion chose, and it would not return to the Land of Whoo. Your mother, Princess Marie, received the powers in this fashion, as the Medallion verified her to be free of malice and pure of heart. She had a vision to help in the desperate struggle of good versus evil in the Land of Whoo."

"Wow," exclaimed Michael Henry, "I believe I *am* the Chosen One. Let's get started with the trials!"

THE FIRST TRIAL
Power of Light over Darkness

Jonathon took the Medallion from around his neck. "Michael Henry, take the Medallion and hold it in the palm of your right hand." He rested his hand on Michael Henry's shoulder to temporarily transfer the power of the Medallion to him.

Michael Henry did as directed. He felt a power come over him with a comfortable warmth. Without uttering a word, the Medallion gave him directions. "Michael Henry, you have done well in finding me. First you must prove how you would use my power without malice toward any man or creature. Show me how you would use the power of light over darkness. You may start now."

Michael Henry spoke without hesitation. "Jonathon, we need to move to an open window in the tower. Quickly, please." They exited the door and moved up the narrow stairway to the first door, next to where Michael Henry had been held captive before he escaped. As they entered, Michael Henry sealed the door so it did not show an opening anymore. Just a wall remained. "Medallion, I wish to use the power of light over darkness."

"As you wish," the Medallion answered in his mind.

The warm sensation continued, giving him a very positive feeling about his whole situation. He opened his backpack and removed the small rocket launcher and a round red rocket with a three-inch fuse attached. "Medallion, I request the power to magnify the light and sound from this rocket as I shoot it over the Crystal City. I also wish to magnify my voice as I shoot the rocket."

As before, the Medallion answered, "As you wish." Jonathon still stood behind him with his hand on his shoulder.

Michael Henry stretched forth his right hand. With a voice magnified and vibrant, his words echoed across the sleeping Crystal City. "Wake up! Wake up, citizens of the Crystal City! I am Michael Henry, the Chosen One, and I wish you no harm. I only seek peace between all people and creatures in the Land of Whoo." His voice resonated as he repeated the message a second time with the same intensity as before. "As a signal, I will send out rays of bright light and loud explosions to convince the Dark Wizard and Master Uror to set our citizens free. I do not wish to rain down fire on the Crystal City and destroy it. I only want to show you the power of freedom over oppression."

He lit one of the rockets with the lighter from his backpack. He hoped that the citizens had never even heard of fireworks, never mind seen them. The rocket exploded with a loud bang over the city, the sound magnified and reverberated as the citizens stood outside their homes and watched in amazement. The bursts of red flashes were also magnified many times over, filling every inch of the city before falling harmlessly to the ground. The citizens ran for cover.

Michael Henry lit a second rocket and repeated, "I am Michael Henry, the Chosen One, and I wish you no harm. I only seek peace between all the people and creatures in the Land of Whoo. I do not wish to rain down fire on the Crystal

City and destroy it, only to show you the power of freedom over oppression."

His voice reverberated on the Crystal City's walls, and the loud bang woke all who were still sleeping. They hurried to their windows to see what was happening. The Dark Wizard, on hearing the commotion, rushed to the tower room where he had left Michael Henry, but saw no sign of him. He immediately deployed his guards to find where Michael Henry was hiding. Most of the Dark Wizard's troops had gone into hiding after the first two rounds of fireworks showered the city, raining bursts of color from the sky.

Master Uror had just arrived and looked sternly at the Dark Wizard after hearing Michael Henry's reverberating voice and seeing the rain of fireworks. "Dark Wizard, you have failed your master. Locate Michael Henry immediately and hold him for my review. You let Princess Marie escape from the Crystal City; you will not make that mistake again with her son. Is that clear, Dark Wizard?"

"Yes, Master," replied the Dark Wizard as Master Uror turned and stormed out of the room, heading back to the Castle of Providence to step up his invasion plans for the Castle of New Providence without delay. He did not completely trust the Dark Wizard to carry out his instructions.

As Master Uror was leaving the Crystal City, he again heard Michael Henry's resonating voice and saw his brilliantly magnified bombardment of color. The message and the explosions went on every twenty minutes until he'd used his last rocket. Then he delivered a final message. "I am Michael Henry, the Chosen One, and I seek peace. I ask you to immediately burn down the ramparts you are constructing as a sign to me that you also want peace between our people."

Before the Dark Wizard's men could be found, the citizens on the ground, fearing for their families, set the ramparts on fire so they could not be used to attack their neighbors in the Castle of New Providence. Michael Henry's voice came again above the growing screams of the people. "Unlock the gates to the dungeons and release all of the Dark Wizard's prisoners and the families of your neighbors from New Providence. Open the gates to the Crystal City to allow anyone held captive to escape."

The Dark Wizard was furious. However, amidst the confusion and fearing that their city would be set ablaze by the raining fire, the citizens reacted quickly to Michael Henry's instructions. They opened the dungeons and gates to allow anyone to flee who wished to do so.

The Medallion came alive around Jonathon's neck and communicated to him and Michael Henry. "I am well pleased with you, Michael Henry, after your first trial. You used minimal powers along with your own ingenuity to save many oppressed citizens in the Crystal City. I have felt their suffering all these years that I have been in such close proximity. Now let's move on to the next trial. Do you wish to start your second trial now?"

Michael Henry answered that he needed to check on Savannah and his grandfather before continuing. "You may have a short break to check on your family," the Medallion said. "Signal Jonathon when you are ready to resume your trials."

Michael Henry reached for his walkie-talkie. "King Titus, Queen Coreen, are you there?"

"Yes, Michael Henry, we are both here." It was not very good reception, and the unit crackled as he spoke.

"How are you, Grandfather? Is all well in New Providence?"

"Yes, Michael Henry, we are well."

"How is Savannah?"

"She is safe also."

"I am working on my five trials for the Medallion and will get back with you later in the day. This is Michael Henry, signing out." He turned to the messenger. "Jonathon, inform the Medallion that I am ready to continue with my trials."

THE SECOND TRIAL
Power of Strength Over Weakness or The Ring of Aiden
The Medallion communicated with both Michael Henry and Jonathon, its words as clear as if they had been spoken out loud. "Your next trial, Michael Henry, is to retrieve the Ring of Aiden from the dragon's lair. You will go to the lair of Gaza, the Slayer Dragon, located in the Mystery Mountains, and recover the ring. Take Jonathon with you so the trial may be authenticated."

Michael Henry again used his walkie-talkie to call King Titus. He asked the king to give Savannah the walkie-talkie. He told his friend to go to the sled and fly to the tower window in the Crystal City before the Dark Wizard's troops could organize and find a way to recapture him. Next he got out his yellow crystal and asked Princess Marie for her wisdom. "Mother, my next trial is to recover the Ring of Aiden from the lair of Gaza, the Slayer Dragon. Do you know anything about this ring?"

Princess Marie explained, "Michael Henry, I am proud of you, my son. My father, Count Aiden, was very outspoken when the warlord Master Uror and the Dark Wizard formed their alliance, which they said was for the good of the people and creatures of Whoo. My father could see through this subterfuge, and he entrusted your father, Prince Knox, with his family ring when we were wed. He explained to Knox that it would give him strength over weakness as he fought bravely for the people and creatures of Whoo. When the Medallion identified me as its primary candidate, it acknowledged that my father, Count Aiden, had acted without malice toward all peoples and creatures of Whoo, and that he had been killed in one of the early battles of the war, defending the kingdom. This was shortly after my wedding. The Medallion had been searching for my father;

after his death, it found me and entrusted me with its powers all these years.

"So you see, my son, the Ring of Aiden has a special meaning for me and also for you. I believe its power had a profound impact on your father's ability to be a brave and courageous warrior for his people, and it also assisted him in becoming a charismatic leader. Once I learned of his battle wounds in the Battle of Providence, I immediately rushed to his side, knowing that the power of health over illness was granted by the Medallion to the one who possessed it. Very sadly, your father, had already perished prior to my arrival. I was heartbroken when I realized I was too late.

"I looked on his hand for the Ring of Aiden, but it was missing from his finger. There were dragon tracks by his side leading to the woods nearby, through the bodies of many of our countrymen who had lost their lives in this fierce battle to save our kingdom. I do not believe the Dark Wizard or Master Uror ever knew of the ring's powers. I can only surmise that the Medallion knows of its powers as well."

It was a lot for Michael Henry to take in. "Thank you, Mother. That explains so much. How should I get the ring back from the dragon?"

"Show no fear. Go to his lair and ask him politely to return the Ring of Aiden. Explain the importance of the ring to what is going on in the kingdom. If that does not work, you will need to do battle with him to regain the ring."

"Michael Henry! Michael Henry!" called a familiar voice from outside his tower window. He looked out to see Savannah on the sled, thankful that he was the only one with the ability to see the invisible sled and that this rescue would stay undetected.

"Thank goodness you are okay, Savannah!"

"I'm fine. Let's go before we are discovered!" He placed the crystal in his backpack and ran to the window. As he jumped from the tower window to the sled, he yelled back to Jonathon to hurry. Jonathon took a flying leap and landed on the sled next to Savannah. Michael Henry was already in the driver's position. He told his crew to hold on tight as he pushed the handles up and forward. The sled rose above the city, and he steered it back to the Castle of New Providence and his grandfather, King Titus. He circled the castle, landing on the king's balcony, and instructed Jonathon to stay on board.

Michael Henry raced in to the king's quarters, followed by Savannah. "Your Majesty, I have just escaped from the Dark Wizard and Master Uror's grip. Before I left, the Dark Wizard told me there was a plan for a surprise attack on your castle. He was building ramparts in the streets of the Crystal City in preparation for battle. His plan was to take them out of the gates in parts, completing their assembly once they were closer to the Castle of New Providence. I have destroyed most of them, but the danger is grave for you. I must be off to complete my trials for the Medallion, so I trust you will take whatever measures you feel necessary to protect your kingdom. I ask to be excused, Your Majesty, to complete my trials."

The king raised his hand to his bowing grandson. "Go with my blessing, Michael Henry, and be safe."

Michael Henry and Savannah ran back to the sled. "I must leave to continue my trials for the Medallion," he said. "Savannah, you would be safer here at the castle, but if you wish, you can come with me. The choice is yours."

"I'm going with you. Let's go!"

As Jonathon and Savannah jumped onto the sled, Michael Henry took his place at the controls. He looked at his friend, and they gave each other a thumbs-up. The sled rose quickly and sped off, headed for the Mystery Mountains and the lair of Gaza, the Slayer Dragon.

Michael Henry felt the sled react to his every move. He told his passengers to hold on while he did one loop-the-loop and then another. *This sled is amazing,* he thought as he sped to the Mystery Mountains. As he got closer, he commanded the sled to land one hundred yards from the entrance to the lair of Gaza.

"Why do they call Gaza 'the Slayer'?" Michael Henry asked. Jonathon responded that Gaza was known to have worked closely with the Dark Wizard and Master Uror at the beginning of the war. There had been talk that Gaza had been responsible for the death of Michael Henry's father, Prince Knox. After Knox's passing, Gaza had not been heard from or seen leaving the mountains.

Michael Henry picked up his backpack and took out the two poisonous crystals he had used on the giant condor back on Earth. He hoped there was enough venom left to do the job, if it was needed. "Savannah and Jonathon, I wish for you to stay in the sled while I go to try and talk with Gaza. If I am not back by sunset, follow these instructions: Jonathon, bring the Medallion for support. Savannah, move to the entrance and listen for the walkie-talkie in case I need your assistance."

Savannah understood the severity of the situation. "Okay, Michael Henry." She wished him good luck as he stepped from the sled.

Michael Henry entered the lair of Gaza, the Slayer Dragon. There was a disgusting smell, with smoky, hazy air that was permeated with a putrid odor of decaying meat. "Gaza, Gaza! This is Michael Henry, the Chosen One, calling you."

Gaza filled the entrance with flames as Michael Henry ducked behind a rock ledge for protection. "Yes, Michael Henry, son of Prince Knox and Princess Marie. I do not wish to speak with you."

"Why not? I have travelled a long way just to meet you, Gaza."

"You are not fooling this dragon, Michael Henry. You only wish to steal the Ring of Aiden from me."

"Gaza, I am calling you out! Come forward," demanded Michael Henry.

"How dare you talk that way to me!" roared Gaza as he filled the entrance with flames and smoke again, sweeping his long tail back and forth while thumping the ground to emphasize his power.

"Gaza, I mean you no harm. I have no malice toward any person or creature in the Land of Whoo. My father was wearing the Ring of Aiden when he fell in battle. When my mother, Princess Marie, came to his side, the ring was gone. I understand you have it in your possession."

"Yes, I am in possession of the Ring of Aiden. You cannot have it. I will defend it to my death—or better yet, to your death!" Gaza lashed with his tail as he lunged for Michael Henry, hissing and filling the chamber with flames as Michael Henry ducked behind the ledge again. Michael Henry clutched the poisonous crystals, one in each hand. Gaza lashed out as Michael Henry jumped away from the sweep of his tail again. Gaza's tail whipped his left hand, throwing the crystal across the cave entrance just as Michael Henry jumped on top of the ledge where he had been hiding.

Gaza did not see Michael Henry jump through the smoke-filled chamber to retrieve the fallen crystal. Relying on his senses, the dragon swept his long tail under the rock ledge. He filled the space where Michael Henry had been hiding with flames, thinking he could snatch up a tasty lunch as Michael Henry tried to escape.

Michael Henry saw Gaza's shadow as the dragon filled the space under the rock with flames. He sensed his chance to strike and dove onto Gaza's head. The dragon tried desperately to shake Michael Henry from his neck, and Michael Henry landed with a thump on the hard ground. "Michael Henry, you are mine!" Gaza hissed, and bent down with his mouth open wide to finish him off.

Then Michael Henry jumped up, the poisonous crystals in his hands. He lunged toward Gaza with the crystal at a sideways angle that allowed it to go under Gaza's heavy scales and enter the skin directly above the dragon's heart.

Michael Henry sensed Gaza's pain and hesitated to push the crystal in its full length. "Gaza, what happened when you found Prince Knox during the Battle of Providence?"

"Your crystal is making me dizzy!" Gaza mumbled, and he fell to the ground. "Master Uror had laid a trap for Prince Knox. His archers shot him in the back. I saw this and felt it was not a fair fight. I watched as Master Uror had the Dark Wizard attack Prince Knox with a hologram that looked like your mother. As he drew closer, a deadly poison came from the hologram. The Dark Wizard reached down to take the Ring of Aiden from Prince Knox just as I slapped my tail on the ground. The ring fell from the Dark Wizard's hand. I grabbed it with my front claws and there it remains. Michael Henry, I can sense I do not have much time left. Let me be."

"I wish you no harm, Gaza. Swear allegiance to me and to the forces of King Titus for the good of the people and creatures of Whoo, and I will spare your life."

"I swear," the dragon responded.

Michael Henry withdrew the poisonous crystal and proclaimed, "From this day forward, you shall be called Cornelius, the dragon who holds no malice toward any person or creature in the Land of Whoo."

Cornelius let out a gigantic dragon roar, shooting a fifteen-foot flame from his mouth. "Michael Henry, I feel like a new dragon, like a weight has been lifted from my neck—like a young dragon again! I have longed to be on the side of good, not supporting the Dark Wizard and Master Uror and their path to destruction. I am honored to fight for justice by your side, Michael Henry, now and in the future."

"I'm sure your desire to fight will be granted very soon."

Cornelius removed the ring from his small claw and gave it to Michael Henry, who reached out to accept it. He felt an unknown power transfer into his body with a tingling sensation as he placed the ring on the second finger of his right hand. The entire ring glowed, but the "A" on its face shone with a brilliance not seen in many years. Cornelius turned his head so he would not be blinded by the light.

Jonathon felt a power transferring from Michael Henry to the Medallion and then back again. Then the Medallion announced to Michael Henry, "I am well pleased with your first two trials. Now I request that you return to the Castle of New Providence and get some rest. In the morning we will resume the trials. Take your new ally, Cornelius, with you. He will be needed in my future plans for you."

Michael Henry asked Cornelius to prepare to depart. As they approached the sled, Michael Henry, Savannah, and Jonathon jumped on board, with Cornelius following close behind. Michael Henry advised the dragon to wait in the large boulders at the edge of the castle grounds when they arrived and said he would signal for him with the flashlight after sunset. This way Cornelius' existence would be kept secret from any spies that might be in the area.

"Very well, Michael Henry, I will do as you ask," Cornelius agreed. Once again, Michael Henry took the controls, and they headed back to the Castle of New Providence.

CHAPTER 7

THE EYE OF THE TIGER

Michael Henry landed the sled and took Savannah with him to see King Titus. The king was meeting with his advisors about plans to defend the Castle of New Providence when Michael Henry arrived in his chambers with his team. He greeted his grandfather with a big hug. "I'm so glad to see you again," said Michael Henry.

King Titus summoned Queen Coreen, and they all discussed the events of the trials. Michael Henry, Savannah, and Jonathon enjoyed dinner with the king and queen, and then they watched entertainers and court musicians in the king's quarters. Michael Henry asked about someplace for his dragon to stay. He told his grandparents how he had changed the dragon's name to Cornelius, and he showed King Titus the Ring of Aiden. The king looked at his grandson with tears in his eyes. "Michael Henry, I am very pleased and proud of all you have done in such a short time. I could not ask for a better grandson. Your father would be so proud of you if he were still alive."

Michael Henry blushed and tried to change the subject as Queen Coreen hugged him, adding her comments of admiration, making him feel very esteemed in her eyes as well. He took his flashlight to the window and signaled

Cornelius to land on the king's large balcony. As Cornelius landed, Michael Henry jumped on his back, and they flew to a secluded area of the castle where Cornelius could rest, eat, and drink to prepare for the next trial. Michael Henry went back to the king's quarters and then retired to a room adjacent to King Titus' room. Jonathon settled into his room located in the same area of the castle. Savannah and Queen Coreen continued to talk about the day's events. Their conversation also included the queen's inquiries about Savannah's family and her life on the farm outside of Marysville. Savannah finally excused herself to her room, situated adjacent to Queen Coreen's chambers.

The first thing in the morning, Michael Henry arose and went to find Jonathon for the beginning of the next trial.

THE THIRD TRIAL
The Quest for the Eye of the Tiger
The Medallion communicated to Michael Henry without speaking a word. "Michael Henry, you have done very well in your first two trials. You have every right to the Ring of Aiden because it was your father's ring. The ring, along with my power, could very well bring you a new level of influence and strength not seen before, finally allowing peace in the Land of Whoo. However, your trials are not yet finished. You have three more to complete.

"The Eye of the Tiger is a petrified eye from a rare white tiger that had powers to see not only into the future, but also to see events unfolding around him, and the ability to see through darkness as if it were light. Some even say that the Eye of the Tiger can enhance one's sense of hearing and reflexes, like a cat. This Eye of the Tiger could be transformed and assimilated into the Medallion, adding its power to that of the Medallion.

"The Eye of the Tiger was last seen in the Desolation Desert. It has an energy signature that some say can be detected by a dragon if the dragon is within one-half mile of the Eye. Once found, you—and only you, the Chosen One—must address the Eye of the Tiger. The Eye will be able to sense your future accomplishments. If it senses a weakness, or sees that you have malice toward any person or creature of Whoo, it has the power to take away your sight. Do you understand, Michael Henry?"

"Yes, I understand," answered Michael Henry. "I am anxious to begin this new trial and continue the vetting process for the Medallion."

Michael Henry bid his grandfather farewell and called Savannah and Jonathon. The three boarded Cuatro as Michael Henry signaled to Cornelius to join them. Knowing they couldn't take a chance that someone would see a flying dragon and become suspicious, he instructed Cornelius to fly alongside them, keeping one foot on the sled to make him invisible. Michael Henry took the controls and steered them towards the Desolation Desert.

Finally, in the late afternoon, they saw an oasis and headed for it. Once they landed, Michael Henry walked towards the oasis. There were several nomads gathering water and setting up their tents. Michael Henry and the rest of his team approached them. "I am Michael Henry, the Chosen One, and I need to find the whereabouts of the Eye of the Tiger," he said.

The men had all heard that the Dark Wizard was offering a reward for Michael Henry's capture. They decided he must be okay if the Dark Wizard was after him. The nomads had never seen a dragon in the Desolation Desert before. When questioned, they did know of a hermit who lived under the Old Rainbow Bridge, a stone bridge with a cave under it. They told him that the hermit was very familiar with the Desolation Desert and may know the location of the Eye of the Tiger. Michael Henry obtained directions to the bridge and navigated the sled in that direction. After they landed next to the arch of the bridge, Michael Henry and Cornelius cautiously moved toward the entrance of the cave.

"I am Michael Henry, the Chosen One, here to see you, sir!"

From inside the cave a voice growled back, "Leave me alone, boy, and get away from my bridge!"

"I am sorry, sir, but I cannot leave unless I talk with you. I require your knowledge of this area of the Desolation Desert. May I interest you in some food and water, kind sir?"

"Michael Henry, I have plenty of food and water, so be on your way."

"We are in a desperate battle with the Dark Wizard and the warlord Master Uror. I must speak with you. I seek information about this part of the Desolation Desert, and I was told you may be able to help me."

"Well, I'll be right out. Why didn't you say that at first?" The hermit emerged from the cave. "My name is Benjamin," he said, extending his hand, "but the locals call me the Snake Skinner. So, tell me about yourself and why you are here—and with a dragon to boot!"

"My mother was Princess Marie, and my father was Prince Knox."

A strange look came over the hermit's face. "I don't believe you. How can you prove what you are saying is true?"

"My mother's favorite color was yellow. She was empowered by the Medallion. My father was killed in a battle for the kingdom many years ago." Michael Henry held his hand out to show Benjamin the Ring of Aiden.

Benjamin sat down on some rocks by the cave. "I served with your father and was there when he fought the Dark Wizard and fell to his trickery. I witnessed your mother, Princess Marie, by his side at the end, trying in vain to save him. After that battle, I lost my will to fight or even to live. I moved to the Desolation Desert, where I have survived all these years on rattlesnakes and desert creatures. I felt like I had let them both down."

The hermit took a deep breath and continued. "I had heard rumors that Princess Marie disappeared after your father's passing and was with child. Since then, of course, the people living in the Castle of New Providence have been predicting that Princess Marie's son would return to the Land of Whoo, and that he would prevail over the Dark Wizard and the warlord Master Uror, and here you are. Unbelievable!"

"Benjamin, what do you know about the Eye of the Tiger that is said to be here in the desert?"

"I am sorry, but I have no knowledge about that of which you speak. However, tonight there could be a caravan passing by the oasis. I trade rattlesnake skins with the nomads in order to obtain my few clothes and goods. We may find someone who has information about the Eye of the Tiger."

"Very well, let's head back to the oasis. You can ride with us."

Benjamin frowned at Cornelius. "What's with the dragon? He looks very much like Gaza, who was an accomplice of the Dark Wizard's for many years."

"This is Cornelius. He did have a relationship with the Dark Wizard long ago, but I trust him with my life now."

"I see. Just let me grab a bundle of skins to trade with, and we can go straight to the oasis."

They headed for the sled with Cornelius close behind. Michael Henry drove Cuatro, and Benjamin got to know Savannah and Jonathon as they flew with Cornelius at their side, landing just outside the oasis. Benjamin walked to the edge of the water and laid out his skins, waiting for those who may want to trade with him. Michael Henry, Savannah, and Jonathon stayed with the sled to remain invisible, while Cornelius flew out over the desert to try again to isolate the energy signature from the Eye of the Tiger.

As the sun sank lower in the sky, nomads appeared from the desert to make their camps around the oasis and, of course, trade with whomever they encountered. As they approached Benjamin, they recognized him from their last trip. They examined the quality of his skins and his collection of rattles. Benjamin addressed them, and as they were discussing the price, he asked them if they had any knowledge of the Eye of the Tiger. They said they had only heard rumors of its existence, but that one of the elders might be over later to trade and may have the information Benjamin sought.

Sure enough, after the sun had set and things started to quiet down, one of the elders came to Benjamin's fire and looked at his collections of skins. Benjamin wasted no time in asking him if he had ever heard of the Eye of the Tiger.

"Yes, of course, but many of my clan believe it to be only a legend," the elder said.

"Where was this Eye seen last?" asked Benjamin.

The elder thought for a moment. "The Eye of the Tiger was located in the Desolation Desert. When its location was discovered by the Dark Wizard, the Eye of the Tiger relocated to the Mystery Mountains, inside the large volcano known as Mount Santiago."

The two men concluded their transaction, and Benjamin returned to the sled and Michael Henry. As he approached the area, he noticed Cornelius returning as well. Michael Henry was anxious to get going and asked Benjamin what he had discovered. The hermit told him what he had heard about Mount Santiago.

"Benjamin, you are free to come with us," Michael Henry said. "If you choose to do so, I would recommend that you first return to your stone bridge and prepare for the journey. We will go to Mount Santiago and return for you on the way out, assuming we are still…never mind. We will see you very soon."

Cornelius had been listening to Benjamin. "Now it makes sense that I have been unable to detect the Eye. The volcano could be hiding the energy signature that can only be detected by a dragon."

"Very well," said Michael Henry. "Let's all head for Mount Santiago. Cornelius, we will meet you outside the volcano." Benjamin waved, and they were off to Mount Santiago.

Smoke billowed from the volcano as they approached. Cornelius dove toward the upper edge but could not sense the energy signature of the Eye of the Tiger. However, he did notice an opening in the side of the volcano and flew toward an area outside this small cave entrance. Michael Henry opted to follow Cornelius and landed Cuatro alongside the dragon. "Cornelius, do you sense anything from the Eye of the Tiger?" Cornelius shook his head. *Very clever,* thought Michael Henry, *for the Eye to hide where we could not detect its hiding place.* He gathered everyone at the entrance to the cave so they could talk about their options.

"I think we should all enter the cave and see what transpires," he said. "Maybe Cornelius will be able to detect the Eye once inside, and we can then use his senses to guide us." He had noticed a stack of small white stones on the ground on the way in. "Let's take the sled back to the stones. We can load some onto Cuatro to use as markers on the dark floor of the cavern so we can find our way out. Even though we have Cornelius and he has expertise in this area, we should be cautious and not leave anything to chance. Better safe than sorry!"

They loaded up the sled with as many small white rocks as they could and headed back to the entrance. As they entered the cave, Michael Henry thought of the powers of the Medallion and directed it to illuminate the cave in front of them, which it did instantly. The team had advanced about one hundred feet into the cave when they ran into a fork in the path. Pointing to the left, Michael Henry called to his dragon, "Cornelius, please go in a short distance and see if you can detect the Eye of the Tiger."

The dragon flew through and came back with nothing. He then entered the right side and let out a roar that all could hear. Returning to Michael Henry he cried, "It's this way! I can sense its presence, and I believe it knows we are here."

Michael Henry checked the supply of white pebbles in his backpack. Savannah had been dropping hers as they entered. He turned towards his friend. "Savannah, you stay here and keep watch while we go in."

Cornelius could sense the Eye of the Tiger so he led the way as Michael Henry followed. As they proceeded farther and farther into the tunnel, Michael Henry grew hotter and hotter. He stopped to drink from his water bottle. As the pair continued, Cornelius suddenly shouted, "Michael Henry, quick, duck under that overhang as I stand in front of it!"

At almost the same instant as Cornelius' warning, a large number of bats flew at them. Cornelius was unaffected by their beating wings and attempts to bite. He let out a roar and a blast of hot flames. The bats headed towards Savannah and Jonathon who, hearing the roar, had instinctively taken cover under a rock ledge as the bats flew out of the cave. Michael Henry gave a thumbs-up to Cornelius.

The Eye of the Tiger unleashed its next surprise. One thousand snakes came slithering toward Michal Henry. Again Cornelius roared and sprayed the ground in front of the snakes with flames, which sent them slithering into any cracks they could find. Just to be sure, Cornelius roared and bathed the cave in flames again as the last of the snakes disappeared into any openings in the walls of the cavern.

"I believe the Eye of the Tiger is ready to talk with us now," Cornelius said. As they approached cautiously, they saw a stalagmite with a figure nested on top.

Quietly, Michael Henry began, "Eye of the Tiger, I am Michael Henry, the Chosen One. I wish to talk with you, if that would be possible."

"Michael Henry, approach with your right hand outstretched and touch the top of my eye. Be warned, if I sense that you bear any malice toward any person or creature in the Land of Whoo, your sight, hearing, and sense of direction will all be removed permanently, and you will have no recourse but to leave my cave along with all who are with you. Do you agree to these terms, Michael Henry, the Chosen One?"

"I agree." He slowly walked forward, his right hand stretched toward the top of the stalagmite. Cornelius nervously thumped his tail on the ground as Michael Henry came closer and closer to the Eye.

"Stop that thumping!" commanded the Eye of the Tiger. Cornelius did as instructed.

Michael Henry continued forward and laid his right atop the Eye of the Tiger. The Eye could not sense any malice toward and person or creature in the Land of Whoo, but was also able to discern the power of the Ring of Aiden.

Michael Henry formally asked the Eye to become part of his team and free the oppressed, standing for good instead of evil.

The Eye had concerns regarding who he would report to. Michael Henry assured him that he would be reporting directly to him and that his services were desperately needed right now. By this time the Eye had ascertained that Michael Henry was all that he claimed to be and was without malice.

The Eye asked the Chosen One, "What if you fail in your attempts to free the oppressed in the Land of Whoo?"

Michael Henry responded that he was the Chosen One and he would not fail, especially with the Eye of the Tiger by his side.

Convinced Michael Henry was genuine, the Eye of the Tiger swore his allegiance to the Chosen One as they looked ahead to their quest and the fourth trial.

CHAPTER 8

TRIAL FOUR - TREASURES TO RECOVER

The Medallion was pleased with Michael Henry's performance so far. The Medallion relayed to Michael Henry, The fourth trial is to recover the Treasures of Eagle's Peak and the Crystal City.

Armed with this new trial, they flew to the stone bridge, picked up Benjamin, and then were off to the Castle of New Providence. Cornelius again waited outside the castle for Michael Henry's signal to come in after dark. Michael Henry had asked the Eye of the Tiger to fly above the Crystal City to listen and observe anything going on, especially any military activity, and then to report back after dark when he signaled for Cornelius.

King Titus and Queen Coreen greeted them as they landed on the balcony. Off stepped Savannah, Jonathon, Benjamin, and Michael Henry. "Come in quickly," said King Titus, "there are spies everywhere in the kingdom!" Even though the sled was invisible, the doorway into the king's residence was not. "Benjamin!" said King Titus. "It has been many years, and I welcome you back with open arms."

After they exchanged hugs and pleasantries, Michael Henry asked, "King Titus, what can you tell me about the Treasure of Eagle's Peak?"

"There have been rumors that Count Aiden's and my son Knox's treasures were raided after the first battles for the kingdom. I do know that when the Land of Whoo was at peace, there was much prosperity for all. My old Castle of Providence held the treasures of our kingdom—thousands of diamonds, emeralds, rubies, artifacts, and gold. Of course, the treasure all disappeared after we were forced from our homes and driven to this remote part of the Land of Whoo."

"And what can you tell me about Eagle's Peak itself?"

"It is always cold and covered with snow and ice. We have heard rumors that the Dark Wizard picked this hiding place for its remote location, and that he lost half of his porters while transporting the treasure to Eagle's Peak because of the extreme weather."

Michael Henry bid all good night and signaled Cornelius to fly in while he would not be detected. The dragon went to his former quarters and bedded down with food and water for the night.

Next, Michael Henry signaled for the Eye of the Tiger to report on any new developments. The Eye began its summary. "The Dark Wizard and Master Uror are both furious about your escape from the Crystal City and have sent troops after the citizens you released. Fortunately, they have all escaped to the woods and are even now forming a militia which will march here to help with the upcoming battle. Master Uror has doubled his efforts to rebuild the ramparts that were destroyed. He believes he must attack within the next two weeks because he is concerned about your growing power. Master Uror has also thrown the Dark Wizard into his own prison for letting you escape, but will release him soon with the wizard's promise not to rest until you are dead."

"Very good. Your report has been most useful. Now, I need you to fly up to Eagle's Peak and look for signs of the treasure we seek. Report back in the morning."

Michael Henry arose the next morning feeling good about his accomplishments so far and experiencing a true excitement about what lay ahead that day. He went into the king's quarters and was greeted by the Eye of the Tiger, perched on the king's balcony.

"Good morning, Michael Henry," said the Eye of the Tiger.

"Good morning. What can you tell me?"

"The Treasure of Eagle's Peak cannot be detected by my sight. However, I did identify a group of one hundred porters heading up the mountain. They have almost reached Eagle's Peak. I was able to listen in on their conversations. They were not happy about how Master Uror was treating them. There were fifty guards in this group. The commander of the guards was talking to his lieutenant and told him in confidence that Master Uror did not trust this hiding place because it was picked by the Dark Wizard, who had let him down recently. Master Uror wanted to move his treasure before someone found out about its existence. The commander said they would need to do away with the porters once the treasure was moved to a more obscure hiding place."

Michael Henry asked the Eye to go back and identify any new happenings while he went to find the king to ask for his advice on his upcoming venture. Michael Henry entered the king's quarters and told him an attack was expected within the next two weeks and that Master Uror was rebuilding the ramparts Michael Henry had destroyed. It appeared Master Uror was going to move his treasure to another location.

Savannah entered the king's quarters, and Jonathon and Benjamin followed shortly thereafter. Michael Henry told them of the events relating to the treasure.

They all talked about what the day might bring while they had breakfast. "I have a plan for my fourth trial to recover the Treasure of Eagle's Peak," Michael Henry said. "I believe Benjamin should stay here with King Titus and take some men to recover the citizens who escaped from the Crystal City. He can bring them back here to the castle to help us in the upcoming battles. Savannah, Jonathon, and Cornelius will come with me when we get word that Master Uror's guards have prepared the treasure for transfer." He turned towards the balcony. "Eye of the Tiger, could this be a trap? There are one hundred porters and fifty guards who can easily be seen from the air. Just to be safe, please make another flyby and look especially for another group of porters or maybe condors keeping guard—anything suspicious or out of the ordinary. Savannah, Jonathon, Cornelius, and I will head to the Star Portal nearby and wait for you there."

They boarded the invisible sled, and Michael Henry commanded, "Home to the Star Portal!" The sled took off like a horse galloping back to the barn after a long trail ride. Cornelius could barely keep up. Once at the Star Portal, Michael Henry went to the rack and secured parkas for everyone. He looked around to see if there were any signs of intrusion, and then shone his flashlight into the portal. "This is Michael Henry, the Chosen One. Has any person or creature attempted to use this portal since I came through here last time?"

"Yes, Michael Henry. The Dark Wizard attempted to leave through the portal with twelve condors and ten specially trained troops in search of you."

"What was the outcome, portal?"

"I informed him that the portal had been locked by you. He tried several spells, and when he was not successful, he finally charged two of his troops to ram the portal to gain entry."

"What was the outcome, portal?"

"Entry was not granted. The portal shut down so he could not communicate any instructions."

"Well done, Star Portal."

By this time, the Eye of the Tiger had appeared at the Star Portal. Michael Henry rose to greet his friend and was anxious to check his hunch.

"Michael Henry, you were right. There was another group of porters and guards on the opposite side of Eagle's Peak, hiding in the snow and in snow caves. I heard some of their animals breathing, which attracted me to their positions."

"Cornelius, you need to fly over the first group of porters and guards," Michael Henry instructed. "Fly close enough so they can see you, yet not so close that their arrows could reach you. See if you can make a roar loud enough to start an avalanche, or slap your tail on some of the high walls of the snow-filled mountains. Look for condors, which may try to attack you from the air or possibly bring messages to the other side of the mountains."

"Very well, Michael Henry. I will return shortly."

"Eye of the Tiger, fly over both groups and listen to their comments about Cornelius. Listen carefully to see if there may also be communications between the groups from the Dark Wizard."

As Cornelius approached the porters in the open area, he buzzed their positions. The guards tried to shoot him down with their arrows. Since the dragon had followed Michael Henry's instructions, he was safely out of range. Two giant condors dive-bombed him from above, but he simply lifted his head and sprayed them both with flames from his mouth and nose. Both birds took off with loud squawking sounds. Out of the corner of his eye, Cornelius noticed a third condor taking off for the other side of the

71

mountain. It flew low to the mountains, barely noticeable. Taking note of his position, Cornelius continued his mission.

Next Cornelius headed for the top of Eagle's Peak and roared at the giant snowy peaks. He slapped his tail on some of the overhanging ledges filled with snow until several avalanches started. The porters and guards took cover and appeared to be safe, but covered in deep snow. This stopped all forward progress and the group dug in for safety. Cornelius repeated the exercise again and again, causing more snow to tumble down the narrow path until the group had no choice but to retreat down the mountainside, away from Eagle's Peak.

Back at the Star Portal, the Eye of the Tiger reported back with the following information: "The troops on the opposite side of the mountain have received communication from a condor. I heard their laughter at how they had fooled Michael Henry, who had sent his dragon after the porters and guards. They think Michael Henry will assume his dragon was successful because the porters retreated down the mountain. Then the condor was off to tell the Dark Wizard of their success in fooling Michael Henry."

"Star Portal," said Michael Henry, "can you transport someone or something to a different location, like the portal by the Four Corners Inn?"

"Technically you should be standing in front of the portal. However, your mother did command me to open up as she was being chased by the Dark Wizard once when she was in the sled, reaching out to transport her and the sled to Earth while she was flying about one quarter-mile from here."

Michael Henry listened with interest and turned back to his informant. "Eye of the Tiger, did you overhear anything else?"

"Yes, Michael Henry. This group of specially trained soldiers must have had condors deliver large sleds to them. Even while some were digging out from the snow, I saw other porters filling the sleds with treasure. They would then ride them down the mountain through the bowl directly below where they are located. They said they were expecting you to leave after you perceived success. There would then be twenty-five condors flying cover over their downhill run, which is slated to start an hour before sunset tomorrow night since it looks like there is a snowstorm coming in tonight."

"Anything else?"

"Yes, Michael Henry. The Dark Wizard was said to have additional condors staged to transport the treasure to a hidden room under the Crystal City where the Treasure of the Crystal City is located. The plan is to combine the treasures so Master Uror can see his entire treasure before splitting it up again. It was repeated that the Dark Wizard needed to gain Master Uror's favor after allowing Michael Henry to escape from the Crystal City."

That was it! This was the news Michael Henry needed. "Medallion, on my signal, I need you to turn light into darkness as the troops start moving the treasure down the mountain." Without any words, the Medallion agreed. "Then, Medallion, I also need your power of reflection and illumination. I will construct a jump with Cornelius' help. As the sleds are airborne, shine their reflections into the Star Portal, which is three-quarters of a mile away."

"Star Portal, can you accept a mirror image to enhance the portal power from three-quarters of a mile away?"

"It is possible, but you should try it now to be sure the distances will compute," the Star Portal replied.

In response, Michael Henry asked the Medallion to send Savannah in the sled from three-quarters of a mile away to the Star Portal. He identified the exact spot and asked Savannah to mark it so, if his plan worked, they would know exactly where to build a jump via their walkie-talkies. Savannah did as he directed her, marking the spot with some black rocks she had brought on the sled. Then Michael Henry commanded the Medallion to transport her directly to the entrance of the Star Portal. He shone his flashlight into the portal and said, "This is Michael Henry, the Chosen One. I wish you to transport this sled through you to the portal through which I first came to the Land of Whoo, the one by the Four Corners Inn."

The portal asked Michael Henry to peer into a small fissure in the rock. He placed his head in the crevice and the portal scanned his pupils for a positive identification.

Michael Henry continued his instructions. "Star Portal, once you have transported the sled through the portal, wait for thirty seconds. Then transport the sled and Savannah back here." He communicated this to Savannah as she verified the exact spot for transfer.

Michael Henry signaled all to proceed, and within a minute those transferred were back.

"Amazing!" Savannah said. "Now what?"

"There is enough room at the portal to hide the Treasure of Eagle's Peak. As we transport the sleds there, Savannah, you and Cornelius will be there to make sure it all fits. Cornelius can help move Master Uror's sleds, if need be. I will be transported there and, with the help of the yellow crystal, seal the portal so no one can find the entrance. Navigating the three sleds from the Star Portal, I will then transport us all back, ending up at the Dark Wizard's treasure site under the Crystal City. We can then move the treasure away from the Crystal City back to its rightful owner - King Titus at the Castle of New Providence.

"Now, Cornelius, can you melt snow with your flames?"

"Yes, of course, Michael Henry."

"Okay. Let's take the invisible sled to the slope so you can see my plan." He drove the sled to the exact spot where Savannah had dropped the black rocks just before she was transported through the portal.

"Cornelius, scratch with your claws and make a pile of snow here on this spot." Michael Henry pointed out the exact location where he needed the snow to end up. "Then I need you to pound the snow down with your tail to make it compact. Where you dug the snow away, you will need to melt the remaining snow, causing it to be very slick as it freezes again." Cornelius signaled to Michael Henry that he understood and would complete his assignment.

"Great, everyone. Tonight, Medallion, an hour before sunset as the snowstorm comes in, can you cause a whiteout so the troops cannot see down the hill?"

"Yes, it shall be done tonight."

The team waited for the approaching storm. An hour before sunset, the Medallion produced a whiteout, and Cornelius worked to construct a wide jump in the large bowl where the sleds would be traveling the next evening. Then Cornelius breathed fire on the snow to compact it. As it refroze, the surface became very slick, and as new snow fell, it covered the work Cornelius had just finished.

"Great job, Cornelius!" yelled Michael Henry. "Let's get back to the Star Portal on the sled."

They all landed safely, and there were now three sleds at the Star Portal. In case there was ever a problem with any given one, another would be readily available. "We will each take a sled back to the Castle of New Providence so all will have a chance to practice driving for the transfer tomorrow," Michael Henry said. Then he turned to instruct the sleds. "I am Michael Henry, the Chosen One. You will follow commands from Savannah and Jonathon as if the commands were directly from me." He drove the lead sled and landed it on the king's balcony. He then directed Savannah to land on the queen's balcony, and Jonathon to land at the fountain inside the grounds. He signaled Cornelius to stay out, as he had done in the past, and fly in when Michael Henry signaled him to do so.

Michael Henry gathered his dream team, including Savannah, Jonathon, Cornelius, the Eye of the Tiger, and Benjamin, who had returned with a group of freed citizens from the Crystal City. They all assembled in the king's quarters for a quick briefing.

"Benjamin," said Michael Henry, "what information did you obtain from the citizens you rescued today?"

"They are very grateful to finally be free. They told me that the soldiers of Master Uror are searching for any of the citizens who escaped. Evidently Master Uror was planning a major push against the Castle of New Providence, and you pushed their schedule back by burning the ramparts. However, Master Uror is working teams twenty-four hours a day to catch up."

He filled King Titus and Benjamin in on the events of his day. He also dispatched the Eye of the Tiger to the Crystal City with instructions to listen in on anything transpiring between the Dark Wizard and Master Uror.

Bright and early the next morning, Michael Henry sought out the Eye of the Tiger for a report on the night's activities. The Eye said it had overheard the Dark Wizard telling an aide to be sure the condors arrived early, assuring all was ready to receive the Treasure of Eagle's Peak, also relaying that he was planning to meet the condors personally. The Eye listened as Master Uror sent a messenger to the Dark Wizard, instructing him to be at his camp outside the Crystal City at sunset to have dinner and discuss the upcoming attack. When the Dark Wizard received the message from Master Uror, he told his treasure guard, Daniel, that after they had finished their dinner, he would bring Master Uror back to show him the combined treasures. He said that Daniel could not leave the treasure depot from now until the condors arrived the next evening.

"Great news!" said Michael Henry.

By this time, King Titus, Queen Coreen, Savannah, Jonathon, and Benjamin were gathered in the king's quarters for a large breakfast. Michael Henry shared his news from the Eye of the Tiger and also informed everyone that he had already dispatched the Eye back to Eagle's Peak. Michael

Henry reviewed his plan of sending the treasure sleds down the bowl, hoping to gain enough speed to get airborne on the jump so they could then be transferred into the portal and secured. Then the sleds—Michael Henry and Jonathon on one, with Savannah and Benjamin following each on their own—would be disguised as the Dark Wizard's sleds.

Michael Henry had already asked the Medallion if it could deposit the troops at the Star Portal from the sleds and then transport the sleds to the portal by the Four Corners Inn with the Treasure of Eagle's Peak. The Medallion had responded, as usual, that this would happen as planned. After breakfast, Michael Henry gathered his team, and they all headed back to the Star Portal where they readied a small, yet secure, enclosure where the troops could be deposited. Savannah was in charge of providing them clothing.

Next Michael Henry took the yellow crystal from his backpack and asked for Princess Marie's thoughts on his progress towards completing the fourth trial. He brought her up to speed. She agreed that the portal would be able to transport them with the help of the Medallion. She warned him that after he completed the trial, the Dark Wizard and Master Uror would be on full alert and the intensity and number of attacks would speed up drastically. "Keep a low profile," she suggested, "and remain humble. Fly the sleds to the wild condors' hunting grounds and bring them back a supply of food, such as small rodents, rabbits, and grain." Her idea was to use this to prepare a feast at the base of the mountain so the extra condors would not mind waiting for sleds to return.

Their plans were in place. An hour before sunset, as planned, the Medallion brought about darkness swiftly. The sleds were ready to start down the mountain with the treasure already loaded, and the signal was given for them to begin.

Halfway down the bowl, the sleds accelerated due to the slickness provided by Cornelius. They took off and the guards held on as they flew over the jump and into the air.

Michael Henry, standing by the Star Portal, shouted the command, "Now!" to transfer the treasure sleds to the portal by the Four Corners Inn. "Remove the troops from these treasure sleds and drop them safely into the secure enclosures at the Star Portal."

Michael Henry, Savannah, and Cornelius were transported to meet the treasure sleds, making sure all the sleds would fit properly in the portal by the inn. Michael Henry used the yellow crystal to completely seal the portal so it could not be seen by anyone, and then asked to transport himself, Savannah, and Cornelius back to the Star Portal, where Benjamin was overseeing the disoriented troops who had just been deposited from their treasure sleds.

"What just happened?" asked the soldiers as Michael Henry arrived.

Michael Henry quickly identified four soldiers approximately the same size as him, Savannah, Jonathon, and Benjamin. He instructed the troops to relinquish their uniforms, while Savannah provided them with replacement clothing. Michael Henry and his team donned their uniforms and boarded the sleds, which were now disguised to look like the troops' treasure sleds. "Cornelius, stay here tonight and get some rest," he said. "Release the troops to make their way down the mountain in the morning and then return to the Castle of New Providence grounds to await my signal tomorrow night."

The team boarded their sleds and were quickly transported back to Eagle's Peak, leaving Cornelius behind to guard the troops at the Star Portal. As planned, the three sleds slid in line giving the appearance they were the first of the treasure sleds needing to be transported. As the condors took each sled in their claws to transport them to the Crystal City, Michael Henry was glad he had instructed the sleds to be covered with tarps so no one could tell if there was still treasure on board. The team dropped bags of food to distract the remaining condors as they were lifted into the air. As they landed, Daniel met the three sleds, accompanied by horse-like creatures to pull the sleds on large, flatbed wagons through the cavernous entrance to the treasure depot. As the sleds were pulled along, Michael Henry, Savannah, and Benjamin again dropped the bags filled with the tasty, disgusting carcasses they'd gathered earlier. The birds immediately stopped all they were doing and started feasting on the meal at hand.

Daniel did not notice the bags being dropped off; he was more interested in telling Benjamin how he could hardly wait to get the mission over with and go to the taverns in the Crystal City. After a fifteen-minute ride in the tunnel, they arrived at the depot. Michael Henry and his team entered with their heads down and scarves pulled up over their faces, as Daniel used his key to open the depot's large secure door. It creaked open, and Michael Henry pulled his scarf from his face saying, "I am Michael Henry, the Chosen One. We are here for the treasure that was wrongfully taken from King Titus and his people!"

Daniel raised his sword but drew back when he saw Michael Henry's team. Daniel spoke quickly. "I have served the Dark Wizard faithfully all these years. I knew that he was taking our citizens for torture and to serve in his armies and did nothing. I wish for change, just like you."

"Swear allegiance to me, Daniel," said Michael Henry, "and we will take you to the Castle of New Providence."

"Very good, Michael Henry. I swear."

"Help us load this treasure onto our sleds, Daniel, and we will be on our way." Michael Henry did not have a good feeling about Daniel. He called on the Eye of the Tiger to help him decide what to do with the wizard's servant. All the while they loaded every last gold coin, but left some of the artifacts behind.

The Eye of the Tiger observed Daniel scribbling a small note for the Dark Wizard: "I will be in touch with you.

They are taking the treasure to King Titus. I am loyal to you, Dark Wizard."

Michael Henry had the sleds in the air, and on the way out of the tunnel he asked Daniel to grab the large painting of King Titus they had left behind. As Daniel went back, Michael Henry raised the yellow crystal and sealed the treasure depot with Daniel inside, leaving the Dark Wizard to try to figure out a way in.

Michael Henry led his group back to the Castle of New Providence and landed on the castle grounds under the king's balcony in plain sight. "King Titus! King Titus! Come and see!"

The king's soldiers were alerted, and all came to the sleds as Michael Henry greeted the king. King Titus ordered his soldiers to move the treasure to his most secure room under the castle. Being a very generous king, he took fifty bags of coins from the sleds and divided it up among his commanders to give out to their men. There was a great celebration that night in the Castle of New Providence, and the citizens all felt a revived sense of hope around their king and his grandson.

Michael Henry went to the balcony and signaled to Cornelius to come to the castle, along with the Eye of the Tiger. They all needed a good night's rest so they would be ready to begin the final trial the next day.

CHAPTER 9

THE FINAL TRIAL

Michael Henry awoke early and went out to find Jonathon. Together they asked the Medallion for the final trial. The Medallion answered Michael Henry alone. "Michael Henry, again you have not only survived, but thrived on your trials. I am well pleased with your progress and await your success on this last trial, which will be to bring Queen Alexis, the mermaid queen, back from the spell of the Dark Wizard. In past trials you have had access to the Medallion in small ways to achieve your success. In this final trial, you will be limited to your own resources and those of the team you have assembled to help you.

"Michael Henry, you must be aware that this trial is the most dangerous for you personally. In order for the spell to be broken, you will need to find Queen Alexis' hiding place and bring her back from the Dark Wizard's spell. Be aware there are markers that will alert him to your attempts, and remember, he is already furious with you for making him look bad before his leader, Master Uror, in your past trials to obtain the Medallion. In addition, Queen Alexis is underwater and access to her and her daughters will be hazardous to you. You are the only one who has a chance of breaking their spell.

"Queen Alexis has the great powers of the seas. The Castle of Providence is bordered on one side by the ocean. An attack has not been possible since the time the Dark Wizard put a spell on Alexis. This is how he won the early battles of the kingdom, by surprising the castle from the sea. Alexis had always guarded against this in the times of peace and prosperity, before the Dark Wizard and Master Uror's alliance against the kingdom.

"The Dark Wizard is unaware that you know of Alexis' existence, and he believes his spell is unbreakable. After all, it has been intact for many, many years. However, the spell can be broken by a single person who has faith that the kingdom can regain its former position of power and has no malice against any person or creature in the Land of Whoo. The biggest challenge of this trial is that if you fail, you will also be under the same incapacitating spell."

"Wow," said Michael Henry, "that's an almost overwhelming challenge for my last trial. Medallion, what will transpire once I have passed it?"

"If you achieve success in the fifth trial, the Medallion will immediately transfer its full potential to you, and you will decide how you wish the Medallion to be available to you. Will it be internalized or worn around your neck? Will it be linked with the Eye of the Tiger, or will you control them individually? Will the Ring of Aiden be connected to the Medallion? Will you immediately embark on saving the Land of Whoo from the Dark Wizard and Master Uror, or will you return to Earth and use the combined powers of these objects to vanquish evil?"

The questions whirled in Michael Henry's head as the Medallion continued. "At any rate, Michael Henry, you will need to complete this last trial before considering the future. Remember, the Medallion will not be available to assist you in any way."

Very well, thought Michael Henry. *I still have my team, Cornelius, the Eye of the Tiger, and the Ring of Aiden as assets - and only one more trial to go.*

He was ready to get going as he called his entire team into King Titus' quarters. "Team, our mission and last trial is to free Alexis, the mermaid queen, from the Dark Wizard's spell."

The king interrupted. "We have all heard that Queen Alexis was killed by the Dark Wizard when he took over the seas bordering the Castle of Providence. She was once one of our most important allies. Her cooperation would be essential for an attack on the Castle of Providence, the Dark Wizard, and Master Uror."

"What can you tell me about Queen Alexis?"

"She was best friends with your mother, and was even in her wedding. We had the ceremony on a large barge alongside the castle at sunset. Marie was so happy, and Alexis was beautiful with her glistening crown of sapphires and brilliant emeralds. The blue gems represented her subjects from the deep blue off-shore waters, and the green stones were for those in the shallower, greener waters close to shore. She was next to the barge, with her tail in the water, shimmering in the golden rays of the sun. Her two daughters, Princess Kelly and Princess Heather, were next to her with their husbands.

"Queen Alexis and Princess Marie had been instrumental in forming the UWL, Underwater League, and the AWL, Above-Water League. They brought together a host of popular athletes to compete for prizes and trophies in the annual UWL and AWL Games outside the Castle of Providence. It was a grand day for all the citizens in the Land of Whoo. The entire royal family was involved. Princess Kelly conducted the sea creatures in the opening fanfare. Her husband, Prince Paul, was very gifted in developing technological advances. Together they oversaw the UWL martial arts competition. Princess Heather's husband, Prince

Benji, was instrumental in training the legions of mermen who, in turn, were always there to defend the castle in the glory days. He also was in charge of recruiting new members for their forces.

"I remember the day of your mother and father's wedding. I was so happy to see my best friend and strongest ally, Count Aiden, give his daughter in marriage. All the mermaids wept as he spoke about his great love for his daughter and his new son, Prince Knox. There were whales, dolphins, and turtles in great abundance, all watching the happy occasion."

"Thank you, King Titus," Michael Henry said. "Knowing that Queen Alexis was so close to my mother and how important she was in protecting the Castle of Providence makes me understand how important it is to free her from the wizard's spell. Does anyone have any ideas?"

Savannah was the first to speak. "I remember seeing a crown with blue and green jewels in the first load of treasure that arrived from the Eagle's Peak."

"Great start," said Michael Henry. "We'll retrieve the crown before we start the trial. Who else has an idea?"

"What about consulting the yellow crystal and asking your mother questions pertaining to Queen Alexis? Maybe we will get some ideas from that," Benjamin suggested.

"Excellent idea!" Michael Henry pulled the crystal out of his backpack. When his mother's hologram appeared, he briefed her on his final trial and asked what course of action she would suggest.

"Michael Henry, after I left your father's side, I went directly to Queen Alexis and told her what had happened. She was very distraught. I finally left the Land of Whoo. Evidently the Dark Wizard sensed Alexis' weakness and took advantage of it with one of his spells. You might find her about five miles off shore, in the Joshua Gardens. These were named for her former husband, who perished in a fierce battle to bring the whales and dolphins into their kingdom and compete in the UWL games. After his death the whale and dolphin leaders pledged allegiance to Queen Alexis, sensing that the Dark Wizard was a traitor to their civilization and would only bring them harm. The Joshua Gardens can be seen from the air as an underwater mountaintop that comes within twenty-five feet of the surface at high tide, and within fifteen feet of the surface at low tide. The gardens should be a brilliant green in a sea of blue water, with a depth of 750 feet, five miles off shore."

"Anything else, Mother?"

"Yes. Be forewarned that this last trial will be very dangerous. I am sure the Dark Wizard has markers to notify him of any intrusions into the Joshua Gardens."

"Thank you, Mother. I will be careful."

"Good luck, my son," said Princess Marie, and her image was gone.

Michael Henry's team was ready for the trial and waited for his instructions. He dispatched the Eye of the Tiger to see what was going on in the Crystal City with Master Uror and the Dark Wizard. Next, he and Savannah took one of the sleds to the closed portal containing the treasure. When they landed, Michael Henry came forward so the portal could scan his pupils.

Once inside, Savannah spotted the crown King Titus had described, dazzling with sapphires and brilliant emeralds. As she placed it on her head, Michael Henry admired his friend with the strawberry-blond hair and fair complexion. Savannah took the crown off and handed it to Michael Henry. He could feel a slight transfer of power from the Ring of Aiden to the crown as the crown illuminated.

"Okay, Savannah, let's take the sled back to the castle and see what else the team has come up with." Before they left, Michael Henry closed and sealed the portal, giving it instructions not to open or even communicate with anyone except him, verified by a pupil scan.

Back at the castle, the Eye returned with more news. Michael Henry gathered the team so all could hear. "Michael Henry, Master Uror has placed a price on your head," the Eye reported. "He has distributed posters saying, 'Wanted Dead or Alive: Michael Henry, who calls himself the Chosen One. REWARD: 10 bags of gold coins and freedom to leave the Crystal City.'

"Master Uror was livid when he found out from a guard that the Treasure of Eagle's Peak had been abducted. He immediately summoned the Dark Wizard, who confirmed that the treasure depot containing the gold he paid his mercenaries had been robbed. The master threw the wizard in jail and did not tell a soul what had happened. He executed the guard who had brought him the news. It seems he was fearful of others finding out that his treasure had been stolen, afraid it would cause rumors that he could not pay his soldiers. Master Uror immediately called his advisors and informed them that they would be attacking the Castle of New Providence within ten days and that there was a reward for Michael Henry. Uror wants daily updates on how the ramparts are coming. He also wants to be informed by his trainers on the condition of his troops. He is combing the area to enforce mandatory conscription into his army. Starting tomorrow, he wants daily estimates of his army's strength in numbers and promises quick executions for any of his captains not bringing in men on a daily basis. They will go to every household in the Crystal City and force the citizens to join the army starting today.

"Michael Henry, every other word is about you and how he wants to have your head served to him on a platter. He will not rest until you are defeated!"

"Eye of the Tiger, did you see or hear of any weakness in the Dark Wizard or Master Uror?"

"Yes. The Dark Wizard was fuming when he was thrown into jail for losing the treasure. I overheard Master Uror commanding his masked torturer to remove the Dark

86

Wizard's left hand as a warning that he means business; that will probably happen tonight. Master Uror seems to not trust anyone and has unleashed a hundred spies who are heading your way to infiltrate the castle. He has also threatened Jasmine's mother and father again and sent her another carrier pigeon. Apparently they were released with the first wave from the Crystal City, but were caught again the day after Michael Henry left due to their infirmities."

Michael Henry had decided his plan of action. "Eye of the Tiger, go to the Crystal City and listen for any mention of Queen Alexis, the mermaid queen, or her daughters, Princess Kelly and Princess Heather. Savannah and Benjamin, let's take a sled to the Joshua Gardens to identify the site and do some research, keeping the sled invisible so no one will spot us." Turning to his grandfather, he asked, "King Titus, do you know anyone who studies the ocean tides around the castle?"

"Of course, Michael Henry. I am on it," said the king.

Michael Henry and his team boarded the sled, made sure they were in invisibility mode, and headed out over the ocean for five miles, hoping to identify the site where the Joshua Gardens rose up from the ocean's floor. As they neared their mark, they saw a large number of dolphins heading for the site and slowed down to watch them. Michael Henry got a hunch and pulled out his yellow crystal. He asked his mother if she had been friends with the dolphins in addition to Queen Alexis. Princess Marie answered that the leader of the dolphins was a bottlenose named Tyler, and that Michael Henry should ask for him. Tyler had been only five years old when Marie left, but as dolphins could live thirty years or more, she advised her son to find out if Tyler was still around. "If you are lucky enough to find him," she said, "direct the yellow crystal at him from less than ten feet away, and I will tell him you are my son."

Michael Henry slowed the sled and skimmed the surface just above the large school of bottlenose dolphins.

"Tyler…Tyler…? This is Michael Henry, the Chosen One…I must speak to Tyler." He repeated the same message as loud as he could again and again. No luck. He was about to pull the sled up when a mature bottlenose dolphin jumped in his direction. Michael Henry hovered just over the water and removed the invisibility feature. He waited for Tyler.

Tyler swam cautiously closer and closer to the sled. When he was within ten feet, Michael Henry pointed the yellow crystal at him. Princess Marie was able to communicate with him as he swam closer to the sled. Understanding now who Michael Henry was, Tyler finally put his nose on the sled, and Michael Henry fondly petted his new friend. Princess Marie told her son to trust Tyler, to jump into the water with both hands outstretched, and Tyler would come to give him a ride as he held on to his dorsal fin.

Without hesitating, Michael Henry jumped in and did as he was directed. Tyler gave him a short ride to the resting place of Queen Alexis and her daughters as Michael Henry looked for any markers the Dark Wizard might have installed to detect his presence. As he drew near, a pulsating noise came to his ears. The school of dolphins instinctively swam around the marker as it sent a message back to the wizard.

Michael Henry intuitively touched the face of Queen Alexis with the finger that bore the Ring of Aiden and thought, *Queen Alexis, this is Michael Henry, the Chosen One, and I will be back to set you free.* He thought he saw a small smile on her face as they turned and Tyler swam back to the sled. Tyler dropped Michael Henry off and waved at him with his flipper. Michael Henry pointed the yellow crystal at him, and Princess Marie thanked him. Michael Henry told Tyler they would be back very soon.

He shivered as he sped back to the Castle of New Providence and landed. He quickly changed clothes and came to stand by a warm fire. Then he went back to King Titus' quarters and gathered his team, including the Eye of the Tiger, who had just arrived back at the castle.

Michael Henry updated his team on what had happened during the search for the Joshua Gardens, and then asked the Eye of the Tiger for a report. As usual, the report was very informative. "The Dark Wizard was just released from the prison of the warlord Uror. He is very distraught over the loss of his left hand as punishment for losing the Treasure of Eagle's Peak. A marker had been set off close to the Joshua Gardens, and a condor was dispatched to verify what was going on. On his return, the condor reported that he had seen a large school of dolphins swimming in a circle around the Gardens, leading to the assumption that there must be a school of fish in that area again. The Dark Wizard basically ignored the signal this time."

Michael Henry thanked the Eye for his report and told the others, "We are going back right away. Savannah, we need the crown. Benjamin, gather blankets for those who may be in the water. King Titus, were you able to obtain any information about the tides in that area?"

"Yes, Michael Henry. It appears that for the next two hours there will be a low tide."

Michael Henry turned to his team. "I need all hands on deck! Savannah, you will go in one sled with me. Benjamin, you pilot another, with Cornelius flying alongside. Eye of the Tiger, you will need to go back and listen for any news and report it immediately to us at the Joshua Gardens. King Titus, I need two expert archers for each sled with plenty of arrows in case we are attacked by condors. Do you have four archers who can be trusted?"

"Yes, I know just who to send with you," answered the king.

"Savannah, we need some small fish as rewards for the dolphins. Check with the queen and see if she can tell you where to get them. We will also need some food for the condors in case they attack us. Benjamin, I need you to find a small platform—say, a four-by-four wooden affair we can strap on the sled to use when we are hovering over the Joshua

Gardens. Make ready, everyone! We will be leaving in fifteen minutes."

Michael Henry boarded the sled with Savannah and two archers and landed next to a small platform that King Titus had provided. With Benjamin's help, he tied it to the sled. Savannah had the crown they'd brought back from the Eagle's Peak treasure. The first sled was off. Benjamin followed close behind, carrying the small fish and food for the condors that Michael Henry had requested, along with the other two archers. They sped to the Joshua Gardens and looked for the school of dolphins and Tyler. Michael Henry hovered above the water and deployed the small platform. He immediately called for Tyler, realizing they were just above the spot where Queen Alexis was entombed. Michael Henry consulted the yellow crystal and asked his mother to communicate with Tyler that they were bringing Queen Alexis' crown back to her, and that Michael Henry, the Chosen One, was going to be able to release her from her spell.

As Tyler approached the makeshift platform, Michael Henry pointed the yellow crystal at him and again jumped in the cold waters. Tyler swam by Michael Henry's outstretched arm as Michael Henry grabbed a hold of the dolphin's fin, holding the crown firmly in his other hand. Tyler brought Michael Henry directly in front of Queen Alexis. Michael Henry touched her again with the Ring of Aiden and placed the crown on her head, concentrating his thoughts at her: *Queen Alexis, for the sake of your daughters, Kelly and Heather, come back from the spell of the Dark Wizard. We need you.*

Michael Henry was out of breath. Tyler brought him to the surface to draw a deep breath and quickly dove down again. Michael Henry put his hands on Queen Alexis' forehead and thought, "*I am Michael Henry, the Chosen One. I have no malice for any person or creature of Whoo. Come back from the spell of the Dark Wizard. We need you.*"

Queen Alexis was just starting to focus and realize what she needed to do as Michael Henry surfaced. As he climbed onto the platform, the Eye of the Tiger alerted him that the markers had gone off and condors were on the way. Michael Henry immediately told Savannah to throw condor food out on the water and alerted the archers to take aim as the huge birds neared. He gave his orders with an authority he hadn't known he had. "Cornelius, as soon as the condors have tried to get some of the food, swoop down from the cloud bank and sweep them with flames! Archers, take aim at them as well!"

The condors approached and, as planned, once they saw a possible meal on the surface, they swooped down to the water, talons outstretched to retrieve the tasty morsels scattered about. They never noticed Cornelius above them, breathing down fire as the archers took aim. The group of four condors quickly fell into the ocean. However, in all of the excitement, the team did not notice a fifth condor which had been in the low cloud bank. Once he spotted the bird, Cornelius quickly turned around and dove at it. The condor was faster and more nimble than the dragon and slipped away towards Providence.

Michael Henry sent the Eye of the Tiger to see if the last condor had made it. Cornelius had given a valiant chase but finally had to break away after singeing the birds' tail and wing feathers. Michael Henry jumped back in the water and again, with Tyler's help, approached Queen Alexis. It appeared she was moving and trying to smile at him. He put his hands on the forehead of Princess Kelly and then Princess Heather, and delivered the same message. *Princess Kelly,* he thought, *I am Michael Henry, the Chosen One, and son of your friend Princess Marie.* And then he approached her sister, Princess Heather, repeating the same thoughts.

Tyler brought Michael Henry back to the surface for air. As he gasped for a quick breath, Michael Henry realized how thankful he was for the low tide. By this time, the Eye of the Tiger had returned with the news that the Dark Wizard was on his way with twenty condors, so the team must be ready.

Out of a bank of clouds, the condors attacked. Cornelius and the archers fought bravely as the Dark Wizard looked for Michael Henry on the sleds. From the small platform, Michael Henry called to Benjamin and Savannah, "Make the sleds invisible, and let the archers and Cornelius take care of the condors!"

It looked like they were winning the battle. Then, as Michael Henry was still trying to revive Queen Alexis and her daughters, the Dark Wizard spotted him beneath the surface of the crystal clear waters. As Michael Henry broke the surface to catch a breath, the Dark Wizard placed a paralyzing spell on him so he would sink to the bottom. Even as the Dark Wizard saw his condors being destroyed, he still believed he had prevailed as Michael Henry sank to the bottom of the ocean. He quickly headed back to the Crystal City to report his success.

Savannah and Benjamin jumped from the sled into the water, right next to Michael Henry's sinking body as it disappeared from sight. They dove time and again searching for him, but with no luck. He simply was nowhere to be found. Savannah yelled across the water to Benjamin, "Let's get back on the sleds and dry off." Once on the sled, Savannah, shivering and sobbing, pulled the crystal from Michael Henry's backpack and said, "Yellow crystal, Michael Henry is missing! What should we do?"

Savannah called for Queen Alexis to come and help them. As a last resort, Savannah grabbed the yellow crystal and threw it in the water, pleading, "Princess Marie, please save Michael Henry!" When Queen Alexis finally surfaced, she was holding Michael Henry, the yellow crystal glowing in his hand. Her daughters, Princess Kelly and Princess Heather, were swimming slowly in their direction.

"Michael Henry," said Queen Alexis, "I sense no malice in you toward any person or creature in the Land of Whoo, and I thank you for bringing me and my family back from the spell of the Dark Wizard."

"And I thank you, Queen Alexis, for saving me from the spell of the Dark Wizard as well," Michael Henry said. Then he asked the queen for her help in attacking the Castle of Providence very soon, and also for safe passage for troops to attack from the ocean side of the castle.

"I will help you in any way you require. Just ask. Now I must go to the rest of my family and free them, just as you have set me free."

"We must all be diligent not to let the Dark Wizard or Master Uror know that I have survived. We can now plan the attack on the castle with the Medallion's full support. Let's return to King Titus and Jonathon and tell them the good news."

With Michael Henry and Savannah riding on one sled and Benjamin steering the other, Cornelius flying closely at their side, the sleds were in the invisibility mode. As before, Cornelius stayed outside the castle grounds to be sure not to alert any spies in the castle. As Michael Henry arrived, the Medallion was close to him and communicated with him. "Michael Henry, you have passed the five trials, and my powers are now one hundred percent available to you. Your mother, Princess Marie, can be very pleased with you."

Michael Henry thought about the coming battle and was acutely aware of what lay ahead of him. As his thoughts swirled, he and Savannah joined King Titus and Queen Coreen in celebrating his victory in freeing Queen Alexis.

CHAPTER 10

ALLIES FOR THE UPCOMING ATTACK

Michael Henry slept in and got out of bed wondering about the full powers of the Medallion when combined with the Ring of Aiden, Cornelius, and the Eye of the Tiger. He was still groggy when he sensed the Medallion communicating with him. He listened carefully.

"Michael Henry, you have done well in achieving victory in all five trials. You now have access to the full powers of the Medallion. How do you wish to proceed with the transfer from Jonathon to you?"

Michael Henry thought, and his thoughts were communicated to the Medallion. "I am focused on the impending battle to save the kingdom from the evil forces. I wish for Jonathon to remain your messenger and for me to learn the full powers as we move forward. Then, after we have defeated the Dark Wizard and Master Uror, my training will be completed with your guidance. Every day you need to communicate with me in the morning, as we have done today, and help me plan our attack using the power of the Medallion. Instruct Jonathon to stay close to me, just as he did during the trials."

"Remember that the Dark Wizard will be very hard to beat—he is livid over your success so far, and his anger makes him dangerous. But you may be able to use this anger against him. I suggest we continue to inflame him and make him look bad in the eyes of his leader, Master Uror."

"How do we do this without the Dark Wizard using his powers against us?"

"If I am in close proximity to the Dark Wizard, he can sense my powers. If I fully transfer my powers to you, this will also send out a signature to alert him. You have chosen wisely to have Jonathon continue as an intermediary. This will also promote the idea that you have perished at the hands of the Dark Wizard."

Before leaving his room, Michael Henry took the yellow crystal out of his backpack. Immediately Princess Marie appeared in a hologram, saying, "Michael Henry, I am very proud of you and your accomplishments. You must realize that the full power of the Medallion comes with breathtaking responsibilities. This will undoubtedly change your life forever. Michael Henry, I understand there have been others who could not deal with the power the Medallion possesses and have had a mental breakdown shortly after receiving its full powers. So use this power wisely, my son. I believe you will make the right decisions, just as you did during the five trials. Now it is time to make a plan to regain the Land of Whoo and free the oppressed. You have attained the full power of the Medallion, and remember, I am always here to give you advice."

With that, Michael Henry got dressed and headed to King Titus' quarters. His team was already fully assembled, having breakfast with the king and queen. He thanked everyone personally for their support during the trials and advised them that they had much to do over the next weeks, with the attack on the Castle of New Providence imminent.

Jonathon was the first to speak up. "Do you still want me on the team? I assume that with the Medallion's powers going fully to you, there will be no need for my services as the messenger."

"Jonathon, during the trials, we all made a great team. I am still learning about the Medallion. I would ask that you continue in your role as messenger for now. Let's do first things first and develop the best plan to free the oppressed and bring King Titus to his rightful place in the Land of Whoo."

Savannah was the next to speak. "Michael Henry, the Dark Wizard believes you are dead. What are your thoughts on how we should handle this?"

"Well, I think he should keep on thinking I am no longer a threat, and maybe we can even help him solidify this belief. King Titus, will you write a note that can be copied by your advisors relaying to the citizens of Providence the following message: 'Greetings, citizens of Providence and the Crystal City. Your Master Uror is out of money and cannot pay his mercenaries. Listen for my signal to free the oppressed and finally bring peace back to the Land of Whoo! Signed, King Titus.' Let's write something like this and have two hundred copies made. Tonight we will have Cornelius drop them over the Crystal City and the Castle of Providence while all the people sleep."

He turned to his trusted team members and continued. "Savannah and Benjamin, let's take the sled with Jonathon and the Medallion back to see Queen Alexis. We will need her help, along with her daughters', to win the kingdom back."

They jumped on the sled and headed for the Joshua Gardens and Queen Alexis. As they had done before, they called for Tyler, and he swam quickly to join his returning friends. They asked him if they could speak with Queen Alexis. Tyler disappeared into the beautiful waters of the Joshua Gardens with a high jump out of the water. Shortly thereafter, Queen Alexis and her daughters swam up to the sled. Soon dolphins and whales were swimming around the sled as well.

"Your Highnesses," Michael Henry said with a deep bow, "I am pleased to see you fully reclaim your throne, and I come to give you thanks and praise for your rightful glory. We have access to some of the treasures that the Dark Wizard has stolen from you. If you care to travel with us, we can lead you to where your treasures are being kept so you can recover the pieces that are yours."

Queen Alexis was very touched. "Michael Henry, you are very generous. We wish to ask Princess Heather to accompany you, since she has always been the most fashionable in our seas. She is also the youngest and can survive out of the water longer than I." As the Queen finished speaking, Princess Heather used her large tail to jump on the sled.

Michael Henry raced to the Treasure Portal by the Four Corners Inn. He used the yellow crystal to unseal this portal so Princess Heather could examine the contents inside.

"Michael Henry, you have done well in collecting all of these priceless artifacts. I see several that were once in our possession."

"Princess Heather, just say the word and they will be yours again."

"Well, those small crowns," she said, pointing to two glistening tiaras, "with the emeralds, they were once worn by myself and Princess Kelly."

Savannah immediately retrieved them and watched Princess Heather put hers back on her head. One could sense the happiness in her voice and eyes. Princess Heather continued, "I also see two rings that were once worn by Prince Paul and Prince Benji. They are the ones with the insignia on the front that shows the royal seal of Queen Alexis. They were used to seal correspondence so all would know it was from the royal family. I also see a stack of royal robes in the corner with sparkling gold inlays along the edges. The royal seal of our kingdom is monogrammed in their silver linings. These were fashioned by our sea creatures and presented as gifts at coronations, including my wedding to Prince Benji and Princess Kelly's wedding to Prince Paul."

As Savannah collected the beautiful robes, Michael Henry asked, "Anything else, Princess Heather?"

The princess took another look at the treasure. "No, I do not see anything else… oh, wait just a minute! I can see the top of another crown that is slightly larger than my mother's." Savannah identified what the princess was looking at and brought it forward. Princess Heather recognized it as the crown worn by her father, King Joshua.

Michael Henry pulled out his yellow crystal, and the sled moved out of the portal. He gave the now-familiar instructions and asked if anyone had tried to contact the portal. The portal replied that both Master Uror and the Dark Wizard had tried, and when the portal had given no response, they had sent condors to look for the opening. Even the condors had not been able to find it after the yellow crystal had sealed it. The Dark Wizard had ultimately tried an opening spell that was not successful, but given time, the portal said, he would figure it out.

Michael Henry closed the portal and gave additional instructions for it not to open or communicate with anyone except the Chosen One, verified by the pupil scan. He also initiated another layer of security by commanding the portal that from now on, it should turn itself off unless it sensed the signature of the yellow crystal, followed by the words, "Princess Marie sends greetings through this yellow crystal. Open only to Michael Henry, the Chosen One." This would allow for another layer of protection which should be good for a few more weeks at least.

The sled returned to the Joshua Gardens and dipped towards the crystal blue waters. Princess Heather used her powerful tail to enter the water, carrying the crowns and rings she had retrieved from the treasure room, and presented them to her mother. Then Tyler made several trips to the sled to collect the royal robes and presented these to the queen. Queen Alexis called Princess Kelly and Princess Heather forward and formally presented their crowns with her blessings for a full and happy life. Then Queen Alexis called Prince Paul and Prince Benji to receive their rings from her. After this, Tyler presented the robes that had been made by his fellow sea creatures to the royal family. The brilliant waters churned from the sea creatures' excitement as they witnessed the royal family once again taking their rightful place as leaders of all who lived in the oceans of Whoo. As the formal celebration drew to a close, Queen Alexis took King Joshua's crown and placed it on his statue in the center of the Joshua Gardens, asking all the creatures to keep it safe. Each and every sea creature acknowledged their commitment to do so.

Next Queen Alexis turned to Michael Henry with tears in her eyes. "You have brought joy back to my kingdom where there was only sadness. How may we assist you in your struggle with the Dark Wizard and Master Uror?"

Michael Henry replied that it was his pleasure to see the entire undersea kingdom united once again, and yes, he would be very grateful for a few favors.

"We are here to assist with anything you need," said Queen Alexis.

"Well," Michael Henry started thoughtfully, "the Dark Wizard believes he has killed me with the spell he placed over me. You were able to revive me with your powers, Queen Alexis. To perpetuate this belief, could you take this shirt I was wearing when he put the spell on me and make it blood-drenched, adding some holes as if I had been attacked once I fell to the bottom of the sea? Then be sure it gets to the shores by the Castle of Providence. If a school of dolphins led by Tyler could deliver it, I would be assured the Dark Wizard would hear of the shirt and know it was mine."

Queen Alexis agreed. "This shall be done. What else can we do?"

"I wish our nations to work together again, as in the past, and I ask for your support in transporting and keeping our troops safe. We are planning to attack Providence from the ocean side of the castle."

Queen Alexis' response came quickly. "Michael Henry, we also wish for the freedom of your people and will support you in any way we can. We will schedule a team of dolphins to stay in the Joshua Gardens as we rebuild our homes. Contact Tyler or his assigned team member any time our help is needed."

Michael Henry thanked the queen as Tyler took a squadron of dolphins to the shore by the castle. They swam and jumped until they were noticed, and then let the shirt drift in. Tyler could verify that a guard had picked it up.

By this time Michael Henry was back at the castle and had again entered the king's quarters with his team. He asked the Eye of the Tiger to fly over the Castle of Providence and the Crystal City to ascertain what plans were being made for the upcoming attack.

"We need to take one of the invisible sleds and hover over the training grounds of the Dark Wizard and Master Uror twice a day," Benjamin added.

"Great idea, Benjamin, but you need to be careful that the Dark Wizard does not sense your presence." Michael Henry brought out the yellow crystal and asked Princess Marie if the Dark Wizard could sense the presence of a sled or of Benjamin.

"Yes, Michael Henry," replied Princess Marie, "I believe that the Dark Wizard has the capacity to sense Benjamin's presence. I suggest you ask the Medallion to enable the sled he is taking to camouflage its signal to the Dark Wizard, and also to give the pilot notice if he is detected."

Michael Henry used his thoughts to communicate with the Medallion. "How can you camouflage the sled and provide a warning to Benjamin when he does a flyover of the Dark Wizard? Surely the Dark Wizard must be using a heightened security alert process now."

The Medallion replied that the Cuatro sled they usually used had been camouflaged at one point by Princess Marie. Because of this, the Medallion could now enable a marker that identified when the Dark Wizard had a lock on the sled, and the sled would then immediately fly out of range and back to base. The occupants would need to be strapped on tightly at all times to ensure their safety, however, if and when this happened.

"Medallion, can you also camouflage Cornelius from the Dark Wizard when he delivers the flyers from the king tonight?"

"Yes, Michael Henry. He will be protected on a one-time basis. Permission will need to be established for each trip."

"Great. Benjamin, you are clear to take Cuatro and hover over the Castle of Providence and the Crystal City. Also search the woods for any remaining citizens we could enlist for our army." Benjamin boarded Cuatro on the king's balcony and they sped away.

Next Michael Henry turned to the messenger. "Jonathon, I need you to prepare questions on a twice-daily basis for the Medallion to help us understand its full power, things that I may not be aware of. I need an update after dinner tonight as we gather for our briefing."

Michael Henry continued around the room. "King Titus, can you please send out communications that we will need citizens to volunteer for a mission to save the kingdom. We will also need you to provide a support team of your most trusted officers to start training these citizens immediately. And finally, I need you to leak word that I have not returned from a dangerous mission at the Joshua Gardens, that you fear the worst but still have hope for my recovery.

"Queen Coreen, please give the same message to Jasmine about my being missing. See that she transports it with a note on a carrier pigeon to the Dark Wizard. Also supply details that I was last seen sinking from a spell that had been placed on me by the Dark Wizard, and that I could not be found after an extensive search of the Joshua Gardens."

Michael Henry now addressed his team. "Savannah, Jonathon, and I will go to the Treasure Portal by the Four Corners Inn and do a preliminary inventory of the treasure. We will seek out a better hiding place that will be more secure from the Dark Wizard. Let's all meet back here at sunset with updates."

Michael Henry, Savannah, and Jonathon took a sled and headed for the Treasure Portal. "Medallion," thought Michael Henry, "I need you to camouflage any device or sled or creature that I am on, shielding my existence from the Dark Wizard. I also need you to set up a force field to prevent him from placing spells on me or my passengers."

"Done," replied the Medallion.

Once at the Treasure Portal, Savannah started organizing the contents with Jonathon, while Michael Henry took out the yellow crystal. "Princess Marie, we need a safe place for the Treasure of Eagle's Peak. Are there any other portals or caves that you have used in the past that are unknown to the Dark Wizard and Master Uror?"

"Michael Henry, my son, you have done well, and I am well pleased with your accomplishments. There is a place offshore from the Joshua Gardens where Prince Knox and I went to be alone right after the conflict started. It is a tropical island with sandy beaches, palm trees, pounding surf, and an active volcano. Coming up from the base of the volcano are large rooms created throughout the ages as the lava forced its way down the mountain. We used to explore the rooms with the help of the Medallion. I called this incredible retreat Grace Island, as it was truly a place of beauty and loveliness."

"Thank you, Mother," said Michael Henry. "Medallion, at my command, transfer the sleds filled with treasure along with myself, Savannah, and Jonathon to Grace Island. Be sure to camouflage us and provide a force field for our protection." Michael Henry sensed his answer: the Medallion understood and would comply.

After two hours of preliminary cataloguing, with the help of the Medallion, Michael Henry, Savannah, and Jonathon had separated the treasure into like items for each sled: rings and chalices onto two sleds; gold bars and coins to another three sleds; then another two for diamonds, rubies, emeralds, and sapphires; with one remaining sled for miscellaneous items. Then Michael Henry gathered his team on Cuatro, engaged the Treasure Portal with his yellow crystal, and ordered the transports to Grace Island. As they left, he closed the Treasure Portal so it could not be accessed by anyone, just as he had done before.

Once on Grace Island, Michael Henry took his sled to the rooms described by Princess Marie. He used the yellow crystal to secure these lava rooms and then had the Medallion transport the treasures there. Using the crystal again, he sealed the entrance. He also had the Medallion place a camouflaged, undetectable force field at the entrance to the lava room. The team took the sled back to the beach. Behind them, flowing down the rocky slope of the mountain, was the most amazing waterfall Michael Henry had ever seen. They stopped for a brief moment and enjoyed the incredible sight, scooping up a refreshing drink from the pool below the falls. Then it was time to jump back on the sled and hurry back to the Castle of New Providence before sunset.

Arriving back at the king's balcony, Michael Henry saw the Eye of the Tiger. He asked for a quick report.

"The Dark Wizard was overheard rejoicing to Master Uror that you had been killed," the Eye said. "Then a soldier came to them carrying your shirt with what appeared to be bloodstains. Master Uror gave the Dark Wizard a high-five in recognition of his accomplishment, but reminded him that you had slipped away before. Master Uror recommended sending spies to the Castle of New Providence to confirm your demise.

"Within thirty minutes, the Dark Wizard returned to Master Uror with the carrier pigeon letter from Jasmine. The message confirmed what they had been told, that Michael Henry must be dead since he had been missing and not seen since his encounter with the Dark Wizard. Master Uror then commented, 'That will suffice for now, Dark Wizard, but you still need to send your spies to confirm.' The Dark Wizard agreed and left to dispatch spies to the castle."

"Eye of the Tiger, you have done well," said Michael Henry. "Return again in the morning and give me another report tomorrow. But first, stay for our sunset briefing with the team, please."

He heard a sled land on the balcony and saw Benjamin returning. Benjamin related that Master Uror had been very busy, soliciting one hundred troops every day into his slavery camps to supply his army. The citizen soldiers were very close to a total mutiny, yet they continued to serve.

At sunset the team gathered for dinner with King Titus and Queen Coreen. They discussed the leaflets that Cornelius would be dropping over the Castle of Providence and the Crystal City after midnight, when the citizens would all be asleep.

Michael Henry filled the team in on what he had learned from the Eye of the Tiger and Benjamin. As they discussed their progress, Benjamin added that the ramparts would be ready within the next two days and that all plans were being finalized.

Realizing it was essential to attack now, Michael Henry turned to his grandfather, "King Titus, make your troops ready."

CHAPTER 11

FINAL PREPARATIONS

Michael Henry awoke early as usual and consulted with the Medallion. The Medallion thought he was still on track with moving the treasure to Grace Island and with his activities last night to continue to inflame the Dark Wizard and Master Uror.

Today will be the day we start our offensive against them, Michael Henry thought. He went to Cornelius and was very pleased to learn his leaflet-dropping mission had gone well the previous night. Next he met with the Eye of the Tiger, who had overheard a messenger delivering the news about the flyers to the Dark Wizard, even including a copy of the flyer. The Dark Wizard had immediately ordered a search for the delivery method. This time the camouflage was successful for Cornelius. A messenger arrived from Master Uror demanding to know how these flyers had been delivered, ordering the troops to find and destroy all they could. However, the message had already been delivered and was spreading among the troops and citizens.

"Master Uror is asking for updates on the ramparts," the Eye continued. "They will be ready for transport to the Castle of New Providence by tomorrow morning. They are planning to move them out of the Castle of Providence gates tonight in readiness."

"Thank you, Eye of the Tiger," said Michael Henry. His team had gathered for breakfast with King Titus and Queen Coreen, and Michael Henry filled them in on the apparent success of last night's events while they enjoyed their meal.

Benjamin was the first to speak in response to the overview. "Being a military man, I suggest an attack on the Castle of Providence tonight with a small but well-organized contingent of troops to force them to move their forces to the Crystal City entirely."

"What do you recommend, Benjamin?"

"Let's bring in teams by sea tonight. When they are moving the ramparts out of the gates, we can attack them. Even if they get the gates closed, we can use their ramparts against them in the attack. They have not posted guard teams on the ocean side of the castle for years because of their success in neutralizing Queen Alexis and her family. Also, we should ask Queen Alexis for her help today in transporting troops.

"In addition, let's bring in archers. With the sleds' invisibility feature, we can take out their sentries and plant our archers in their place on the crenellations of the castle. We also need to use the sleds to transport troops to the woods outside the castle to help support the attack on the ramparts and to keep the gates from closing after the ramparts are moved out."

Michael Henry informed Savannah and Benjamin that he would need them to start transporting troops after those going by sea were delivered to Tyler's team of dolphins. "We will all take Cuarto to visit Queen Alexis today," he said. "King Titus, we will need a hundred of your best men ready for transport at sunset, along with one hundred expert archers—and be sure the archers are dressed in black clothing."

Jonathon then spoke up. "Michael Henry, most of Master Uror's forces train outside of the Crystal City, and most of the Dark Wizard's men are stationed at the Castle of Providence. Once Master Uror senses the castle is under attack, he could send literally thousands of troops to their defense. If we have not secured the castle, his troops will surely overwhelm us. However, their weakness is in the old wooden bridge that crosses the Smokey River, which they must cross to provide assistance to the castle. We could tar the bridge and have Cornelius set it on fire as we start the attack."

"Excellent idea, Jonathon. King Titus, how do we get a supply of tar?" King Titus immediately sent for an advisor to look into locating the tar.

"Medallion," Michael Henry thought, "we will need a camouflage again tonight for Cornelius and for all of the sleds as they deliver our troops."

Michael Henry advised his team to meet him again at noon for lunch to discuss their progress. He asked Benjamin to take a sled under camouflage to the Smokey River to identify troop strength and any other details. The unusually heavy fog around the river in the early morning and evenings would certainly help ensure the success of this mission.

Michael Henry, Savannah, and Jonathon took Cuarto to visit the Joshua Gardens and again called on Tyler to help locate Queen Alexis. She appeared within a few minutes with a warm greeting for her friends in the sled. "How may I help you?"

Michael Henry replied that tonight at sunset they would be delivering troops on their sleds to the Joshua Gardens, and asked if Tyler and his team could ferry them the five miles to the coast of the Castle of Providence where they would stage their attack. Michael Henry explained that his sleds could hold ten soldiers each and that they would make several trips if she could provide dolphins for the trip in.

"That's a great idea, Michael Henry, especially as we have discovered that the Dark Wizard has just completed installation of markers on the ocean side to identify sleds or any other flying objects coming in to the Castle of Providence. He believes I am still neutralized and unable to assist in an assault from the water."

Michael Henry steered Cuarto back to the Castle of New Providence and also swept the countryside looking for the spies the Dark Wizard had promised to send. They noticed a band of horsemen approaching the castle, traveling along the main road between the two castles.

After landing Cuarto back on the king's balcony, Michael Henry approached King Titus. He asked his grandfather to send his Special Forces immediately to the spies and try to sign them up for King Titus' army, making sure to comment on the king's sadness on losing his grandson.

As the team gathered for lunch, Michael Henry asked for updates. The Eye of the Tiger reported that the Dark Wizard had been called tonight to Master Uror's headquarters at the Crystal City to review his plans for the attack on the Castle of New Providence, scheduled to start in the next few days. The Dark Wizard was on his way in the carriage provided by Master Uror and had just crossed the bridge over the Smokey River a few minutes earlier.

The next report was from King Titus. His generals had selected a number of troops that were ready to leave for Tyler's team, along with archers and Special Forces to land in the woods near the Castle of Providence.

Cornelius had been listening on the balcony and spoke with Michael Henry. He was ready to do his duty on the bridge.

King Titus proposed to transport a maintenance detail of twenty-five soldiers that would cross the bridge over the Smokey River. They would create a disturbance, causing a distraction that would allow the transported wagon to drop hot tar out of the bottom of the wagon onto the bridge, unnoticed, as they crossed back toward the Castle of New Providence. King Titus commanded half of his troops to defend one side of the bridge and half to defend the other, preventing any passersby from putting the fire out.

"Cornelius," instructed Michael Henry, "once we have dropped the tar from the wagon, we need you to set the tar on fire by shooting flames across the bridge.

"Medallion, use your powers of light over darkness to create a dense fog and keep it up until sunrise."

Michael Henry looked around the room at his team. "Take the afternoon to make your preparations. We must be ready to attack by sunset!"

CHAPTER 12

THE BATTLE BEGINS

Michael Henry addressed his team during an early dinner. "We will need to start transporting troops right away so they are in place." He had just shared the update from the Eye of the Tiger that the gates would be opening at midnight to move the ramparts out of the castle to assemble them. "They plan to start moving them into the woods immediately so they will be ready to start their journey to the Castle of New Providence in the next several days."

Benjamin spoke up. "Michael Henry, our time is now! Let's start moving troops into place by midnight. We are ready to use the ramparts against them if need be. However, if we can catch them with few sentries posted, we can storm the gates, and with the archer support, we can retake the castle before first light."

"Everyone in agreement?" asked Michael Henry. They all nodded. "Very well, let the battle begin! Benjamin, Savannah, and I, along with Jonathon, will start flying troops to the Joshua Gardens and deposit them with Tyler by 9:00 to be transported to the shore by the Castle of Providence. We will then transport our Special Forces to the woods outside the castle by 10:30 so they can set up a command post and secure an area for one large transport by the Medallion." He smiled to himself, realizing he was learning more about his new powers every day.

"Medallion," he thought, "once we have a landing site in the woods, you need to transport the remainder of the troops in one group along with their weapons, horses, and equipment. The sleds will then deliver archers to the crenellations in the castle after making one sweep to remove any existing guards. We must time this to coincide with the gates being opened to allow the ramparts to be moved out.

"At this point, I will ask the citizens to leave the castle as we take it over and secure it. I will let them know that anyone left inside will be considered hostile and dealt with accordingly. During this time, King Titus will supply another unit of two hundred troops, which will be transported in after the grounds are cleared, to go door to door to secure the area. Cornelius will need to be ready, along with the tar wagon and horses, to be transported by the Medallion at midnight to the bridge over the Smokey River."

King Titus stood and raised his glass, proposing a toast. "To the new kingdom of Whoo! Let us go forward and free the oppressed!"

Michael Henry raised his glass towards his team. "Let the battle begin!"

And with that, the plan was set in motion. Michael Henry told Savannah and Benjamin to organize the troops to be transported by Tyler's team as he and Jonathon boarded Cuarto to make sure the team of dolphins was ready for the upcoming invasion.

Michael Henry and Jonathon were at the Joshua Gardens within minutes, calling for Tyler. As Tyler surfaced, the water churned with schools of hundreds of dolphins. The sleds started arriving with Savannah and Benjamin, along with loads of troops ready to be transported to shore.

The sleds headed back to the Castle of New Providence and loaded the first group of Special Forces to find a staging spot in the woods just outside the Castle of

Providence. They landed quickly with the first group and secured the area for the next team. Within fifteen minutes, Michael Henry told the Medallion to transport the group of waiting soldiers with their horses and equipment to this secured area. The last archers boarded Cuarto and the other two sleds, preparing to fly in the invisibility mode over the Castle of Providence, awaiting midnight when the gates would open.

Back on the shores outside the Castle of Providence, the dolphin teams had dropped off the hundred-plus troops. They were readying their equipment as Michael Henry had instructed, but they would not start the attack until the Medallion illuminated the grounds. Then they would rush to the front gates from their hiding places among the rocks along the shoreline. Also by this time, the teams had been transported to the landing area in the woods outside the walls of the Castle of Providence. The horses were a bit uneasy after their strange arrival. However, their riders did a remarkable job of comforting them quickly and quietly, and in no time at all they were ready for battle as they waited in the silent darkness for the conflict to begin.

The main gates of the Castle of Providence creaked open. Michael Henry and Jonathon circled the castle on Cuatro, looking for targets on the highest points on the castle walls. The invisible sled was joined by two more undetectable sleds, one driven by Savannah and one by Benjamin. Within a few minutes the sleds had landed the first teams of archers, who set up strongholds and took the place of the former guards. Between the time the gates had finally opened and the first ramparts were being rolled out, the sleds had delivered additional teams of archers, repeating until all of the archers were in place. Both teams, one in the woods and the other on the highest walls of the castle, had been admonished not to attack until the grounds were illuminated by the Medallion. Interestingly enough, the soldiers on the ground were so busy opening the gates and moving the ramparts out that they did not even look up and notice the additional guards crouching on the tallest structures and walls of the castle.

The ramparts had all been moved out of the gates after what seemed like hours. During this time the wagon at the Smokey River Bridge was permitted to cross, the false bottom allowing the crew to coat the wooden bridge with a thick layer of tar. They could barely see their way across the bridge due to the dense fog. As planned, Cornelius flew over when the wagon was safely on the other side and ignited the tar. The entire bridge was engulfed in flames within a very few minutes. The Dark Wizard's guards could not see the flames due to the dense fog, and when they could finally smell the smoke, it was too late to save the bridge.

Looking down on the Castle of Providence, Michael Henry thought, "Medallion, illuminate the grounds and reverberate my voice now!" Then he made his presence known. "I am Michael Henry, the Chosen One. You cannot win. Throw down your weapons, put up your hands, and run into the woods to avoid certain death. Do it now!"

As expected, many of the oppressed workers immediately ran for the woods as the Special Forces units emerged from their hiding places among the thick trees and from the ocean side of the castle. All the while, the archers picked off the Dark Wizard's troops who had not accepted Michael Henry's invitation to flee and had chosen to stay and fight. Inside the castle the wizard's troops were waking to the castle being overrun by the Special Forces from King Titus and Michael Henry.

One of the Dark Wizard's messengers got off a carrier pigeon with a message. "Return immediately! We are under attack by Michael Henry!"

On receiving this message, the Dark Wizard interrupted Master Uror's meeting with his generals. Uror's face became as red as a beet as his anger rose. He commanded that two thousand troops be awakened and sent over the bridge at the Smokey River to save the Castle of Providence. These troops were to be under the command of his best general, General Owen.

Back at the Castle of Providence, the grounds were illuminated and the archers fired on the Dark Wizard's troops, blanketing the entire area with arrows. Cornelius flew to Michael Henry's position at the Castle of Providence to check in. Michael Henry decided to burn the ramparts outside the castle walls and commanded Cornelius to help with this next stage of the conflict. With flames shooting from his mouth and nostrils, Cornelius added to the commotion and mayhem already taking place. The Dark Wizard's troops were helpless under this tremendous siege as the castle was secured by King Titus' soldiers. Many of the Dark Wizard's troops simply dropped their weapons and stood with their hands in the air as the oppressed citizens ran into the woods.

As Cornelius circled the castle, he noticed a flock of condors flying towards the Castle of Providence. He gave a giant dragon roar to alert Michael Henry. The teams boarded their sleds to intercept these threats with several archers on each sled. Cornelius fell in line behind the sleds in hot pursuit, singeing the condors' feathers as the archers fired upon the birds.

Immediately on his return to the Castle of Providence to wrap up the operation, Michael Henry asked the Eye of the Tiger to go and oversee the Crystal City troop movements and do a flyby on the former bridge over the Smokey River.

General Owen fumed as he neared the Smokey River Bridge. He could smell the smoke from a mile away and could not believe his eyes as they approached. He tried to cross the bridge, only to turn back after just a few feet on the blackened, rocking surface over the rushing water.

"Dark Wizard," Owen commanded, "perform your magic and illuminate the bridge so we can clearly see the damage!"

The Dark Wizard did as he was told, cringing as he viewed the destruction.

General Owen's voice cracked with rage as he screamed, "Dark Wizard, why is my bridge burnt to cinders? How will my troops get to your castle? I thought you said Michael Henry was dead! Use your powers to fly over the castle and return then to tell me the damage so far. Do not fear that Michael Henry will do you harm because if you stay here any longer, I will kill you myself. Go now and return immediately with your report!"

The Dark Wizard quickly flew over the Castle of Providence, only to see his troops kneeling in a corner of the castle grounds with their hands in the air. The gates were sealed and the walls completely secured with troops loyal to King Titus. The ramparts were either on fire or already burned to the ground outside the castle walls.

Michael Henry had set up a warning system with the Medallion to notify him instantly of any foreign presence, such as the Dark Wizard. The Medallion communicated the Dark Wizard's arrival. Michael Henry commanded the Medallion to again magnify his voice and illuminate the sky around the Dark Wizard. "Citizens of Providence, look up and see your Dark Wizard as I illuminate his flight!" he cried. "Next we will capture him to face trial for his oppression!" But before Michael Henry could attack, the Dark Wizard turned tail and headed immediately, but reluctantly, back to General Owen.

"Dark Wizard," General Owen shouted, "what good news do you have for me?"

"I have none, General Owen. The bridge is impassable. The Castle of Providence has been overtaken. My troops are being held captive. And I was almost destroyed in flight when I was recognized before I could complete one quick pass over the castle!"

General Owen immediately dispatched a carrier pigeon to Uror and waited for a reply. His note read, "Master

Uror, your bridge over the Smokey River has been destroyed, and the Dark Wizard's Castle of Providence has been overrun. What are your wishes, my master? Shall the Dark Wizard return with me, or should he pay the price for his stupidity now?"

A carrier pigeon arrived shortly with Master Uror's reply. "General Owen, bring the Dark Wizard back to me with a small force of your men. Assign your second-in-command to take the remainder down the ravine and cross the river, then back up the steep cliff to begin another bridge. I need to cross the river by noon tomorrow, and no later! I am sending carpenters now to assist you."

General Owen immediately assigned his second-in-command to take three hundred troops down the ravine, while the others started cutting down trees near the bridge to allow another bridge to be built.

Back at the Castle of Providence, Michael Henry had debriefed the Eye of the Tiger, finding out he had heard Master Uror's men talking about the urgency of completing a new bridge, which Master Uror intended to cross by noon. Michael Henry sought out Savannah, Jonathon, and Benjamin, along with the original archer teams. Flying in invisibility mode, they headed to what was left of the bridge over the Smokey River at dawn.

Benjamin was the first to zero in on the teams making their way up the ravine. The troops ignored his warnings. *This is like shooting fish in a barrel*, thought Benjamin, as they hovered over the troops in the ravine and pummeled them with arrows. Then Michael Henry took his sled to where the carpenters were starting to construct the new bridge with the recently cut trees. The archers expertly fired blankets of arrows on the soldiers moving the trees. They continued with pass after pass, firing as the troops ran for cover. Michael Henry again had the Medallion magnify his voice as he said, "This is Michael Henry, the Chosen One.

117

Run into the woods for your lives and come to the side of good. Do it now or you will be destroyed!"

The soldiers under the general's second-in-command all looked terrified. Arrows flew from nowhere, and now this Michael Henry was calling the shots! They had also heard the screams of their comrades in the ravine, running for cover as the arrows showered down on them. It was already too late for many of them. The second-in-command yelled, "Retreat to the Crystal City!" as his troops ran for their lives, along with their animals. Half of the troops fled to the woods to escape Master Uror's oppression.

Michael Henry, along with his team and the archers, returned by sled to the Castle of Providence. With Cornelius, they then navigated to the Smokey River to destroy the work of the carpenters and woodsmen by burning the trees that were being used to start construction of the bridge. Cornelius was having a heyday as he burned tree after felled tree. By this time, any remaining troops in the ravine had vacated the area.

A carrier pigeon was sent to General Owen with a message saying, "General, Michael Henry has used invisible archers to attack our positions in the ravine. He then brought in a dragon using flames to completely wipe out our first attempt at the new bridge. We are scattered and our command has been dismantled."

General Owen sent back a reply: "Immediately return to the Crystal City and we will regroup."

Michael Henry observed the troops retreating and then headed back to the Castle of Providence. The Eye of the Tiger was waiting to relay how furious Master Uror was and how he had assembled all of his generals, along with the Dark Wizard, to plan an attack to retake the Castle of Providence. "Master Uror said that you, Michael Henry, are the number-one enemy of his kingdom," the Eye went on. "He has concluded that you must have either spies or a listening device, because the attack on the Castle of

Providence was too well planned. He asked his generals, 'How could Michael Henry know that the gates would be opening and catch the ramparts outside of the castle walls? This cannot be a coincidence or a lucky guess. We have to assume the worst, that we have traitors in our midst.' Uror continued that starting now, any traitor would be executed immediately, and that the Dark Wizard, who is in charge of treachery and secrecy, would be held responsible for losing the Castle of Providence to Michael Henry and King Titus."

Michael Henry remained quiet while the Eye disclosed the rest of its findings. "Master Uror informed the Dark Wizard that he would now be totally responsible for finding the traitors and making sure that no information reaches King Titus or Michael Henry. He was told to look at every means possible, using any treachery he may devise. He is to place markers everywhere in the Crystal City just in case the king or the Chosen One have discovered some advanced apparatus that can listen in on conversations. Uror wants no effort spared, and he told the Dark Wizard that if he fails in this mission, he will pay with his life. Master Uror ended by yelling at his generals, 'You have all failed me, and if I do not see immediate improvements, you will pay the same price as the Dark Wizard! Is that clear?' And they all answered, 'Yes, Master.'"

Michael Henry asked about these markers the Dark Wizard would be using. The Eye replied that they could be very impactful in stopping the daily stealth searches for information. "So why has the Dark Wizard not used these in the past?" Michael Henry asked.

"I have been able to avoid these because they carry a signature that I detected on my first visits. I have just flown out of their ranges. I expect the Dark Wizard will now triple the number of markers and set up additional warning systems, now that they suspect my existence."

"How do you propose we get around these markers?"

"I will do a mile-high flyby now as Uror gets started, and I will set up remote listening stations above the ranges of the markers he will be installing. Then perhaps we can have some advanced warning as to their locations. I will also start sending my army of dragonflies, a hundred at a time, over the Crystal City to rotate every hour on the hour, day and night, and report back to me."

"How long will it take for the dragonflies to be discovered by the Dark Wizard?"

"I would expect that within the week he will notice the dragonflies and cast spells to eradicate them," the Eye answered.

"Can we mix the dragonflies with rodents or other insects so the Dark Wizard does not suspect us?"

"Yes, of course, but the information will return to us much more slowly. However, that idea could work, so today I will release three hundred rodents from my old enclave in the Mystery Mountains. I will place these rodents, with the Medallion's help, in the Crystal City tonight. I will travel there now to make preparations."

Michael Henry conveyed a thought to the Medallion. "You will need to transport these rodents from the Eye of the Tiger's old cavern in the Mystery Mountains. Jonathon and I will travel there and meet with the Eye at midnight tonight to make the transfer." He spoke aloud again. "Eye of the Tiger, what else can we do today?"

"When I go to my enclave, I can also prepare fifty snakes and 250 bats to patrol at night, allowing the rodents quicker access back to me for a faster response. However, I still expect the Dark Wizard to shut down our attempts once he is fully aware of them. I also suspect that he now knows how dangerous you are to him, both physically and ideologically, and that he will be making plans to attack you and anyone who is with you. He will most likely set up measures of a very secret nature to protect himself from Master Uror. He may even plan on eliminating Master Uror using one of his poisonous spells—that would be my guess. This will take a good part of his time in this coming week. He will need to react quickly, before you have time to respond and plan another attack. This is only a guess from my listening activities so far, however."

"Great plans, Eye of the Tiger! Put these in place and tonight at midnight we will launch your teams of dragonflies, snakes, rodents, and bats one at a time so they won't be noticed, aiming them at different parts of the Crystal City."

Michael Henry was now back at the Castle of Providence with King Titus, who had gotten a ride from one of the sleds. His grandfather had tears in his eyes as he entered his old quarters. As he looked around the room, memories of what once was came flooding back, steeling his resolve to free his people and reclaim his kingdom. Michael Henry waited for the appropriate time and related the plans from the Eye of the Tiger. He then called his team together for their first meeting in the king's original quarters. Michael Henry briefed his team on the upcoming missions and congratulated them on a job well done in taking the Castle of Providence back from the Dark Wizard. "Let's have a meal together now and talk about our strategies going forward," he said.

As they ate, King Titus stood to give a toast. "Here's to freeing the oppressed and taking back what is rightfully ours!"

Benjamin asked Michael Henry what he was doing to protect himself, King Titus, and Savannah from a spell by the Dark Wizard. Michael Henry replied that they all needed to be especially vigilant and not take anything for granted. Benjamin added that by this time the Dark Wizard would have learned that the shore on the ocean side of the Castle of Providence was again under the control of Queen Alexis and her family, so it would make sense that he would try to place troops and/or spies on the shores unnoticed. Michael Henry noted this as well and related that he would be taking a trip to the Joshua Gardens to brief Queen Alexis on what had happened and ask for her continuing support.

"Medallion," Michael Henry thought, "do I have the power to provide storm-force winds and waves if an attack were noticed from the Dark Wizard?" He immediately understood an affirmative answer from the Medallion.

Benjamin spoke up again, asking Michael Henry to transport additional troops to guarantee the safety of the Castle of Providence. King Titus confirmed he could muster another thousand soldiers and would put all his troops in both castles on high alert. Michael Henry decided that the transfer of the thousand troops would be made at sunset.

As the group concluded their meal and their conference, King Titus rose and said he would return to the Castle of New Providence to make preparations for the battles to come. Next, Michael Henry and Jonathon boarded Cuarto and headed to the Joshua Gardens to see Queen Alexis. As they approached the sparkling blue water, Tyler swam over to greet them, sending messengers to alert Queen Alexis. After the Queen arrived, they congratulated her family and Tyler's team of dolphins on their excellent job in the battle to retake the Castle of Providence.

Michael Henry briefed Queen Alexis on what had transpired, thanks to her, and also on what they expected to occur as a result. He warned his mother's best friend to be on the highest alert, since the Dark Wizard would surely try to place spells on her and her family again.

Queen Alexis informed Michael Henry that she had already set up an army of remora with special sensors to detect any disturbance in their waters or energy signatures of the Dark Wizard. She had also placed her sons-in-law, Prince Paul and Prince Benji, on twelve-hour shifts leading patrols in their waters on the assumption that there would be another intrusion by the Dark Wizard. In addition, the queen had enlisted an army of poisonous lionfish to attack, on her command, any unknown person or creature in their waters.

As a precaution, the Eye of the Tiger had developed an automatic alert bracelet for Queen Alexis to notify the Eye and Michael Henry of any intrusion into her waters. Once Queen Alexis engaged the alarm, they would provide assistance immediately. If Michael Henry needed support, his bracelet would send an immediate message to both the Eye of the Tiger and Queen Alexis.

Michael Henry landed the sled back at the Castle of Providence and again met with the Eye of the Tiger. The Eye had done a high flyby over the Crystal City on its way back to the castle and noticed additional markers being installed. He even sensed that his presence had already sent a message to the Dark Wizard, so he zeroed in on a conversation between Master Uror and General Owen about the Dark Wizard.

The general related that he had placed twenty-four-hour guards, unnoticed by the Dark Wizard, to keep track of his goings-on. General Owen had sensed that the wizard could not be trusted. He thought that the Dark Wizard was planning an overthrow of Master Uror and might even be responsible for the attacks on the Castle of Providence by allowing Michael Henry to continue undetected, taking the focus off the wizard himself.

The Eye said that Master Uror had then replied to General Owen, "You have done well, as usual, General Owen. Let's start with plans to nullify the Dark Wizard's powers by monitoring his every move and develop a way to use his powers against him. Capture one of his apprentices and torture him until he gives us a potion or some way to accomplish our agenda. Keep this sorcerer in the desert cavern where we have our hidden emergency treasures, where he will be known only to you and me."

Michael Henry knew this information was invaluable. "Great job, Eye of the Tiger. Let's keep a lookout over the desert and listen in when they begin their operations."

Just then he received an alert from Queen Alexis. He and Jonathon immediately flew on the sled to the Joshua Gardens, where the queen met them. She disclosed that a band of ten ships had been launched, and that the prevailing winds and currents would bring them over the Joshua Gardens around sunset. Michael Henry communicated his plan to the Medallion. As the ships approached the Joshua Gardens, a wind storm would arise to prevent the boats from continuing. These winds would need to blow them back to their starting point, no matter how hard they would row. Michael Henry told Queen Alexis he would be back at sunset to address the ships, and then he headed back to the Castle of Providence.

The Eye of the Tiger had already observed General Owen's troops heading into the desert with the Dark Wizard's trainee, Lucas. As they forged ahead, they questioned Lucas about the weaknesses of the Dark Wizard. His apprentice refused to answer. "When my Master finds you out, he will turn you all into flames and ash for your insolence towards him and me!"

"Lucas, you will not live long enough to see this happen," said General Owen's second-in-command. "You must tell us what we ask, or perish. What is the Dark Wizard planning, and how is he preparing his attack on Master Uror?"

"I don't know what you are talking about!"

After a long desert ride they settled in a cave, and the torture of Lucas began in earnest. But no matter what the soldiers tried, he would not talk.

As sunset approached, Michael Henry and Jonathon neared the Joshua Gardens. Michael Henry thought, "Medallion, bring lightning and winds on my command. Reverberate and magnify my voice now!" He spoke to the ten ships as Tyler's dolphins swam circles around them. "Sailors from Master Uror, we wish you no harm. Turn around now." He waited, but there was no reaction. "My name is Michael Henry, the Chosen One. You are in unauthorized waters that are ruled by Queen Alexis. You must leave now!"

He looked across the water for a response to his command. Still they were steadfast and kept moving forward. He spoke to them again. "This is Michael Henry, the Chosen One. We are fighting to free the oppressed. You must turn around now or face immediate destruction from my powers!"

Still there was no change in their course. Michael Henry thought, "Medallion, start your winds and wave actions, and we will return to the Castle of Providence."

Once back at the castle, the Eye of the Tiger was ready with another report. General Owen's troops had dug in and tried to gain information from Lucas, but with no luck yet.

"Medallion," thought Michael Henry, "give me a report on the wind and sea conditions at the Joshua Gardens." The reply came swiftly: there were forty-knot winds and fifteen-foot seas as the ships headed back to their base. "Very good, Medallion."

Midnight approached and the Medallion transported additional troops to secure the Castle of Providence. With the castle secured, Michael Henry was content that all was well. He looked forward to a good night's rest, and in the morning, he and his team would start to plan their attack on the Crystal City.

CHAPTER 13

THE DARK WIZARD FIGHTS BACK

The Dark Wizard toiled all night producing poisonous gasses, placing them in capsules that could be carried by his fleet of condors and then released over the Castle of Providence. Secretly he also placed some of the mixture into a hologram of himself that could deliver a dose to swiftly kill any person or creature looking at the hologram from a distance of three feet or less. This was the same gas he had used to destroy Prince Knox, changing the tides of the war so many, many years ago. As he stirred the mixture, the Dark Wizard thought of a time in the future when he could unleash this hologram on Master Uror and finally take rightful control of the kingdom. After all, wasn't HE the one responsible for the many successes over the past decade?

"*Where are you, Lucas?*" thought the Dark Wizard as he continued to produce his poisonous mixtures. He was unaware that Lucas was being held and tortured by Master Uror's troops to gain knowledge to be used against the wizard himself.

The poisonous mixtures swirled above the wizard's cauldron, and he realized something. He was risking his life by producing this caustic mixture. How could he do it without putting himself in jeopardy? Was it time to implement the solution he and Lucas had been discussing for so long? He had wanted his young trainee to be present to witness this moment, but he was still nowhere to be found. The Dark Wizard knew what he must do. He chanted the yet untested spell to release the Spirits of the Underground. Success! Twelve Spirits of the Underground came forward to serve him directly. These spirits could mix the potions, and the Dark Wizard would be protected from harmful exposure. Very pleased with himself, he had another idea. Why not unleash these Spirits of the Underground right now against Michael Henry? If the spirits were successful, he could then release them on Master Uror, exacting his revenge on the taskmaster who had imprisoned him and severed his left hand.

Knowing that these Spirits of the Underground could be hard to control once unleashed, the Dark Wizard set out to test their effectiveness. He called for Lucas again using his best spells, but no luck. Lucas did not return. Was Master Uror responsible for this, or was it just a coincidence? Whatever the reason, it was clear the Dark Wizard would need to proceed on his own, without the help of his apprentice.

The Dark Wizard had taken some of Lucas' clothing and tasked five Spirits of the Underground with finding the person who had worn the articles. "Use any means necessary. Search the entire city to ascertain in which direction he was taken. Your only rule is that you must not be seen by Master Uror."

The five spirits swirled and then howled. With banshee screams, they set off on their search for Lucas. They swept over the grounds swiftly with no luck and then, as if someone had hit the reset button, they all started over, searching for clues again and again. Finally, hours later, these deadly spirits sensed that General Owen's quarters may have been visited by Lucas recently. They entered through the keyhole, recognizing they were on the right track. They were able to determine where General Owen was—in a conference with Master Uror. They waited outside, becoming more and more impatient. Remembering the wizard's instructions that they could not be seen by Master Uror, they listened in to learn what they could.

Master Uror and General Owen were discussing the fact that no progress had been made in Lucas' interrogation. He seemed to be withstanding all forms of torture that they had used thus far. Uror ordered the general to personally go into the desert and oversee Lucas' questioning, and once he was assured he had all the information he could get, he should make certain that Lucas was never seen or heard from again.

"Yes, Master," the general replied, and left for the desert to face Lucas, totally unaware that the underground spirits were now following his contingency of troops.

The Eye of the Tiger met with Michael Henry first thing in the morning, before the team had assembled for their briefing. The Eye had already sensed the Spirits of the Underground and their mission to follow General Owen to find Lucas.

"What powers do these underground spirits possess?" asked Michael Henry.

It was a difficult question to answer. "I am uncertain of their complete powers, since the Dark Wizard has never used them before. They have always been considered very hard to control, with a distinct possibility of turning on the sender. They have also been regarded as very unstable, to be used only as a last-ditch effort. This leads me to believe the Dark Wizard is up against a wall to do or die. The spirits, as we surmise, can travel freely once released from the Underground by the Dark Wizard or whoever controls them; they can group together, as we understand, and encircle a victim, removing the air from their space and suffocating them. However, these characteristics are untested. All we know is theory so far. We also believe that they can take over other creatures or persons and make them do their will."

"What would make these spirits turn on their master?"

"I suppose if they felt or somehow thought that the Dark Wizard was going to send them back to the underworld they could become unstable and turn on their sender to keep from being imprisoned again for an eternity."

Pondering the information, Michael Henry had another question. "Eye of the Tiger, what have you discovered about Master Uror or the Dark Wizard since we last met?"

"General Owen's troops have taken the Dark Wizard's trainee, Lucas, into the desert and are torturing him to reveal any secret spells the wizard may have come up with and to see what plans he has in place to use against Uror. It appears that Master Uror does not trust the Dark Wizard. In addition, we have detected that a number of the underground spirits have been released by the Dark Wizard, and he is using them to help mix his poisonous potions. The Dark Wizard was overheard instructing the condors that they were going to have a mission to drop canisters of his poisonous gasses over the Castle of Providence. Also, Spirits of the Underground have been detected looking in the desert for the secret hideout where General Owen's troops are holding Lucas."

"And what is your opinion of Lucas? Could I go to his assistance and possibly turn him away from the Dark Wizard to the side of good?"

"It is possible. However, the danger would be great. You could be captured by General Owen's troops, or taken by the Spirits of the Underground who seem to be hovering over Lucas."

Michael Henry drew out the yellow crystal to seek Princess Marie's advice. He told his mother of his intention to go to the spirits to show them that, in the end, they would be destroyed by the Dark Wizard, and that they should turn away from him and embrace the side of good. He reviewed how the wizard had been experimenting with having the condors fly poisonous gasses over the Castle of Providence.

Princess Marie understood the severity of his situation. "My son, I know that if it were me, I would attack with all my might. One thing is for certain: your chances for success diminish the longer the Dark Wizard and Master Uror have to consolidate their plans, as I found out through my own experiences. Strike now while you have the momentum. You may also want to search the Dark Portal, if you have not already done so. The Dark Wizard may have left something that could be used against him."

Michael Henry gathered his team to discuss their options and give them an update on what he had learned. He suggested, as his mother had, that they carried the momentum at this point and should attack soon, hopefully catching them off guard again. He then went to the Desolation Desert to visit with the Spirits of the Underground to try to win them over to his team.

Deep in the desert, the spirits had finally located General Owen's troops and Lucas. Lucas, finally broken, was giving up many of the Dark Wizard's secrets, including how he would use his poisonous gasses and how he had planned to bring out twelve Spirits of the Underground. Because he feared he could not trust the spirits long term, he had been preparing a spell to use against them to send them back to be imprisoned underground.

Lucas was unceremoniously executed by General Owen after giving up his secrets, and the general returned to Master Uror.

Michael Henry had decided to take the invisible sled Cuatro to the Dark Portal, which was located near the Crystal City and the Dark Wizard's command post. He called for Savannah and Jonathon to join him. Michael Henry had sealed all of the portals in the same way so his protocol would be in place to gain entrance even though he had never been to the Dark Portal. He could feel its sinister power signature as he approached. He looked at the small opening and entered with his team. As they worked their way to the center, he illuminated the stalagmites and stalactites with his flashlight.

Michael Henry gave his now-familiar instructions to the portal. "This is Michael Henry, the Chosen One. I command you to open and conduct the verification process that has been communicated to you." Immediately the Dark Portal asked Michael Henry to peer into a small crevice as it scanned his eyes to verify his pupils. With a whir, the portal opened. He explored the portal's entrance, leaving it open in case of an attack by the Dark Wizard. If necessary, Michael Henry had planned an immediate escape from the cavern via the Dark Portal.

Michael Henry, Savannah, and Jonathon explored every inch of the massive chamber. Savannah found a canister of some sinister-looking material with a label attached. "Dark Wizard, Poisonous Gas, Handle With Care." There was a folder next to the canister that contained a plan which called for the portal to open and for condors to carry the gas to Earth. The birds were to launch it over any city where Michael Henry was located and virtually wipe out the entire population to be certain of his fate. This plan was to be executed immediately once it was certain that the first condor attack was not effective. Evidently the Dark Wizard had planned on launching the attack just prior to Michael Henry closing down the Dark Portal completely.

Looking around, Jonathon observed a black satchel that he surmised was for the Dark Wizard to use if Master Uror was about to take him out. The ditch bag contained a number of gold coins, diamonds, rubies, and emeralds in a sealed, three-gallon goatskin bag. There were also clothes and another goatskin bag labeled "Potions" that Jonathon did not open. Another, smaller goatskin bag was labeled "Antidotes for Poisonous Gas."

Michael Henry sensed an irregularity in the cavern and immediately closed the entrance. "Run to the portal and enter on my command!" he yelled. "Now! Enter the portal!" As they cleared the opening, he commanded the portal to close and seal itself using his protocols. "Transport us to the Star Portal immediately, and seal this entrance!"

Arriving back at the Star Portal, Michael Henry took a deep breath and said, "That was a close call." He surveyed the portal and felt sick as he sensed something irregular. He looked at Jonathon. "Come and stand by me." Michael Henry somehow could feel that several of the Spirits of the Underground had returned with them through the portal. The spirits must have been waiting in close proximity to enter once they saw Michael Henry come close to the Dark Portal. "Savannah, grab some parkas, get a sled ready for transport, and wait for my instructions."

Just then the three Spirits of the Underground awoke in the cavern and started swirling around Jonathon and Michael Henry. He tried to communicate with them, saying, "I am Michael Henry, the Chosen One, and I mean you no harm. What is it that you wish?" The spirits kept swirling around the pair. Was this what the Eye of the Tiger had told him about? If so, the air would soon be vanishing. Michael Henry thought quickly. "Medallion, make the Spirits of the Underground plainly visible to me. Provide Jonathon and me with a force field that encircles us, allowing air to enter freely while protecting us entirely. In addition, notify the Spirits of the Underground that I wish to communicate with their leader."

"Michael Henry," came a ghostly, raspy voice, "what do you wish to say before you perish at our hands?"

"Spirits of the Underground, I am Michael Henry, the Chosen One, and I mean you no harm. I wish to talk to you about joining forces with my team to upset the power of the

Dark Wizard and Master Uror. I can promise that if you will change to the side of good and swear allegiance to our cause, you will be spared."

The rasping voice barely made a chuckle. "We are the ones in command here, not you! Do you have any last requests?"

Michael Henry thought, "Medallion, I wish for you to turn light into darkness so the Spirits of the Underground cannot see or sense any direction." The Spirits of the Underground rammed into each other in their efforts to swirl around him. "Now, attack if you dare!" They tried in vain to make a run at the pair but instead ran into the force field and each other.

"Medallion," thought Michael Henry, "return the light to our area." Immediately all could see clearly. The Spirits of the Underground took another run at Michael Henry and Jonathon, but with a much greater loss of power than they had experienced before. "Your choice is clear," Michael Henry said. "Do you wish to be imprisoned again in the Underground, never to return, or do you wish to swear allegiance to me now?" All was quiet. "This is your last chance. It's now or never. What is your decision?"

The Spirits of the Underground asked Michael Henry to promise not to imprison them if they changed their ways and supported him. "How will I know you are sincere?" he asked. The leader responded that once they had changed, they would not be accepted by their comrades and would need to return to the Crystal City to engage the other Spirits of the Underground.

"Very well. Do you swear allegiance to me, to have no malice against any person or creature from this day forward, and to abide by the laws I will set forth for you?"

They all replied, "Yes, we do, Michael Henry." As soon as the words were spoken, all the spirits stopped. "We have had a great burden lifted from us by your actions." They turned to look at their liberator.

Michael Henry responded that from this day forward, the three spirits would be called the Spirits of the Portal. He informed them that after their mission was completed, they would guard the three portals to the Land of Whoo. Even though the portals could be sealed, he sensed that in the future their heightened senses would be essential in protecting the Land of Whoo from invasion. He then asked Savannah and Jonathon to prepare the sled as he closed the portal using his protocols, and they all headed for the Crystal City to meet with the other Spirits of the Underground.

Once at the gates of the city with the invisible sled, the three spirits headed out to find their companions and bring them back to meet Michael Henry. Unfortunately, as they had feared, they stood out to their peers, and the other spirits could sense Michael Henry clearly, even as he waited on the invisible sled.

As the sled came to a stop outside the gates, the Dark Wizard's markers alerted him of the intrusion. Sensing Michael Henry's presence on the sled, the wizard swooped down on the invisible sled with a spell that allowed him to see the sled and its occupants. Immediately he dispatched his troops to throw nets on the sled and its passengers. Seeing what was happening, Michael Henry thought, "Medallion, energize your most powerful force field!"

As the conflicting spells took effect, Michael Henry realized the Dark Wizard had placed a spell on the person closest to him in the sled. Savannah was pulled out of the sled by this spell just as this new force field was activated. Michael Henry yelled out to her, and he and Jonathon ran to her within their force field to attempt to break the spell. "Medallion, bring Savannah back within the force field immediately," Michael Henry thought, but she moved only slightly toward Michael Henry and Jonathon. The Dark Wizard was also pulling her away.

Michael Henry sensed the danger to Savannah as she was being torn between the two. "Medallion," he thought, "secretly place a marker that will allow you to track Savannah without the Dark Wizard's knowledge, and wait for my command to leave with the sled. Also communicate to Savannah that she is in danger of being torn between the two forces and that you are placing a marker so we can come back tonight to rescue her." His mind was racing, trying to cover all possible consequences for his friend. "Medallion, can you place a remote force field on Savannah until we return?"

The Medallion's answer was swift. "Yes, Michael Henry, but it can only protect her for twelve hours." Michael Henry communicated to the Medallion to proceed with the plan, and the sled immediately jumped away from the Dark Wizard. Savannah was left behind, a temporary force field surrounding her. The Dark Wizard commanded his troops to take her to his cauldron area where the Spirits of the Underground were concluding the preparation of his poisonous gasses. The wizard was pleased with his new assistants, knowing they could not be harmed by this mixture. He determined that this area would be the perfect place to keep Savannah, where any attempt by Michael Henry to rescue his comrade was sure to fail.

Savannah was terrified as she watched what was happening to her, unable to do anything to stop it. Yet she remained calm as she sensed the Medallion had placed a marker to follow her and that she would be protected for twelve hours from the poisonous gasses being mixed by the Spirits of the Underground. At the entrance to the cauldron area, the spirits took over and led her into the room as she waited for Michael Henry's return. She looked on as the spirits communicated with the Spirits of the Portal that had accompanied Michael Henry back to the Crystal City on the sled. They seemed to be arguing and unable to decide whether to support Michael Henry or not. The spirits that had overheard Lucas confess the Dark Wizard's plan to send them all back to their eternal underground prison had not yet returned to the group, so the argument continued.

The Dark Wizard had taken the extra precaution of sealing his cauldron room so no one could enter or exit without his being aware of it. As a result, even the Spirits of the Underground were locked out once they arrived back at the Crystal City from the desert.

Master Uror had been notified of developments by the Dark Wizard, who felt there was a chance of returning to Uror's good graces if he could lure Michael Henry back and capture or kill him. Master Uror immediately sent additional troops to both support and watch the Dark Wizard. General Owen was told to stay close to the Dark Wizard during this time of uncertainty and to report anything suspicious directly to Master Uror.

Back at the Castle of Providence, Michael Henry assembled his team to tell them the news that Savannah had been captured and that her life depended on their quick and thorough preparations. "What are your suggestions?" he asked.

Jonathon told the group that there was a weakness in their team, and it was him. "What if the Dark Wizard sensed the Medallion is really worn by me, but being commanded by Michael Henry from a relatively short distance? He could separate us and interfere with your ability to command. Could the Dark Wizard or Master Uror use this power of the Medallion against us?"

Michael Henry thought carefully. "You have a valid point, Jonathon. How should we proceed?"

"You should command the Medallion to leave me and be fully operational as it connects to you."

Michael Henry communicated with the Medallion. "What are the dangers in doing this?"

The Medallion replied that the transfer could possibly render him unconscious for a short period of time, but most likely would have no ill effects.

Wanting to look at all sides of the issue, Michael Henry asked, "What are the advantages in doing this?" The Medallion replied that these powers would increase in Michael Henry, but there could be a slight learning curve with the new powers. "What new powers?" he thought. The Medallion replied that it was different for every person, but because of his youth, whatever these powers were, they would be more intense and also enhanced by the Ring of Aiden.

Michael Henry took out his yellow crystal and, with the team gathered, asked Princess Marie what her recommendations would be.

"Michael Henry, you have done well and I am well pleased. Your thoughts of transferring the Medallion to you make sense from a defensive position, as the Dark Wizard would love to separate you and Jonathon if he knew the situation. However, the most dangerous time is when the transfer has been completed. It could impact your judgment and cost Savannah her life. The decision is yours and your team's, but the fate of the people and creatures of Whoo is in the balance. Taking into consideration the real possibility that you and Jonathon could be separated, I feel the Medallion would be safer if you had all the power directly, since you will be challenging the Dark Wizard soon. If he were to separate you and Jonathon, it could be the end of our attempt to retake the Land of Whoo."

Michael Henry thought for a few moments and then turned to his team. "I believe I should complete the transfer. What say you?"

Jonathon and Benjamin were both in agreement that the best course of action was to call for a transfer. Michael Henry communicated to the Medallion, "Proceed with the transfer." To his team he said, "We will proceed with the transfer of power now."

With a blinding flash of light, the transfer was complete, and both Michael Henry and Jonathon slumped to the ground unconscious.

.

CHAPTER 14

MICHAEL HENRY TO THE RESCUE

King Titus had been notified by Benjamin and was now at the Castle of Providence with his grandson, who lay unconscious along with Jonathon after the dangerous transfer of the Medallion. Michael Henry lay in the king's bed as they all watched and tried to determine if he was still alive. His breathing was very shallow, his chest barely rising with each breath. The Medallion was now attached to him as it had been to Jonathon. Hours went by as the team kept vigil around his bed, along with King Titus, watching for any sign of life.

Benjamin had been keeping track of the time. He realized that Michael Henry had been out for over eight hours and that he had been back from the Crystal City for an hour prior to that. That meant that Savannah had around three hours left to live. Her force field would melt away and she would be exposed to the poisonous gasses in the cauldron room where the Dark Wizard had sealed her, according to the marker placed by the Medallion.

King Titus sat by his grandson's bedside, telling him how proud he was of his accomplishments. He told him that

Jonathon was in a bed they had set up nearby. King Titus then spoke to Jonathon, thanking him for his years of service as the messenger for the Medallion. The king looked at him, thinking about the years they had known each other. Jonathon was Michael Henry's uncle—Princess Marie's sister Georgia had been happily married to Jonathon. Princess Georgia had been the maid of honor at Princess Marie's wedding to Prince Knox so many years ago. Georgia had been taken hostage by Master Uror during one of the first battles and executed because she would not bow down to him. Jonathon was heartbroken. Princess Marie had loved her brother-in-law as if he were a brother. She saw an outlet for his talents and asked him to become the messenger for the Medallion to save the Land of Whoo. He agreed. Without this agreement, the Medallion would have been forced to move to an alternate world and find another who was worthy.

Another hour went by. Benjamin watched the minutes tick by. Savannah only had two hours left, and there was no movement from Michael Henry.

King Titus continued talking, turning now to Michael Henry's team. He reminded them how lucky they were to be a part of such great adventures with Michael Henry, and that, because of their efforts, the Land of Whoo was about to be freed from the Dark Wizard and Master Uror.

Benjamin walked over to the bed. "Michael Henry, I do not know if you can hear me, but Savannah has an hour left before her force field will dissipate, leaving her unprotected."

By this time the Eye of the Tiger had returned. He gave his reports to those waiting with Michael Henry and Jonathon. Savannah had been taken hostage and Master Uror could hardly wait for Michael Henry to try to rescue her, since she was in a sealed room where the Spirits of the Underground were mixing the Dark Wizard's poisonous gasses.

That did it! Michael Henry and Jonathon awoke with a start at the same time. Jonathon looked at his leader, friend, and nephew. "How do you feel, Michael Henry?"

"We do not have much time left to free Savannah," he answered. "How do my powers work now that the Medallion has been permanently assigned to me?"

Jonathon inquired if Michael Henry could get out of bed, and Michael Henry decided to find out. He was a bit wobbly, but made it to the window. He pulled out the yellow crystal to ask his mother for advice. But Princess Marie couldn't give him the answers he sought.

"I sense your added strength, Michael Henry. When the powers of the Medallion were transferred to me, I was only unconscious for two hours. However, I was older than you and had not worked with the Medallion as you have."

"Do you have any idea how these powers will affect me?"

"Well, my son, you will not really know until you try them and push them to their limits. The power of strength over weakness and the transport powers will probably work for you directly. I became aware that the more you ask for, the more you receive, so go rescue Savannah and return safely."

Michael Henry put the yellow crystal away. "Eye of the Tiger, what is your latest update?"

"The bats have just forwarded news to me from the rodents, snakes, and dragonflies. We believe the cauldron room is completely sealed off, including the window. The spirits in this room are upset that they are not free and seem to be imprisoned again. The spirits you befriended in the desert are outside the sealed room, trying to figure a way through the wall that is protected by the wizard's spell. These spirits agree that the Dark Wizard must be overthrown for them to be safe again. They feel certain they will be imprisoned again.

"One very interesting piece of information came from the rodents and snakes. There seems to be a secret tunnel that is now sealed leading from the stairway going to the tower. This tunnel comes out at the cauldron room. There are no signatures or markers set by the Dark Wizard in this tunnel. It is about four feet wide and filled with rodents and bats. They led my rodents and snakes to an eroded wall that can be accessed by small creatures on the north section of the tower, twenty feet below the Dark Wizard's quarters."

"Medallion, I need to rescue Savannah and only have forty-five minutes left. Transport me to the cauldron room where she is and unseal the room, producing a force field around both of us."

Michael Henry stood by the window, the Ring of Aiden glowing with a brilliant light. He bid his team goodbye, along with his grandfather. "I must test the Medallion's powers, since it has aligned with me now, and rescue Savannah—and I must do it quickly. Wish me luck! Medallion, transport me to the Crystal City."

The Medallion communicated that Michael Henry should jump from the window. "Put your faith in me," it said. Michael Henry dove out of the window, and shot like a rocket to the Crystal City.

"I want to do a steep loop and then up, followed by a steep dive down," he thought. The response was just as he had anticipated: immediate. Then he thought, "I want to enter the eroded wall to allow access into the tunnel, exiting at the cauldron room. Surround Savannah and me with a force field."

He entered the wall and instantly followed the tunnel with the guidance of the Medallion, crashing through a wall that had once been a doorway many years ago. Without stopping, he grabbed Savannah and screamed, "Hold on!" He traveled back through the tunnel and continued to the Castle of Providence with Savannah in his arms.

Back at the castle, he dropped off Savannah. "No time to talk now. I must return to the Crystal City." He again dove out of the window and zoomed back to the tunnel.

The Dark Wizard was waiting for Michael Henry to return. He tried throwing fire bolts and every spell he knew as Michael Henry approached, but he was unable to stop the Chosen One. Michael Henry again entered the tunnel and went directly to the still-sealed cauldron room. Using the same tunnel, the spirits had gained access to join their comrades. All twelve Spirits of the Underground were now in the cauldron room, waiting for Michael Henry. They had sensed his entrance through the tunnel.

The Spirits of the Underground addressed him. "What are your intentions?"

"I am Michael Henry, the Chosen One, and I mean you no harm. If you swear allegiance to me and hold no malice toward any person or creature in the Land of Whoo, I promise to treat you fairly and justly. What say you?"

They all answered in unison that they swore allegiance to him. Sensing their resolve, he said, "From this day forward, you will *all* be called the Spirits of the Portal. I will station you on both sides of the portals, on the side of Earth and the Land of Whoo. From now on, you are not to allow access to anyone except me or those accompanying me to protect both Earth and the Land of Whoo from aggression." This would allow the spirits their freedom and also help to protect both the Earth and the Land of Whoo.

The spirits asked about different scenarios. What if they found an aggressor like the Dark Wizard—how could they both defend themselves and turn back the aggressor?

"Great question," answered Michael Henry. "You will have a force field from this day forward"—he conveyed the thought to the Medallion—"which will protect you from the Dark Wizard and those like him. The only one who can break this force field will be me. You can place yourself in the path of the aggressor, and they will be unable to pass.

You, of course, will keep your abilities to swirl around a target and remove the oxygen from this person or creature. You must follow all the protocols of the portal that have been set up by me. Is that clear?"

"Yes, Master," they all replied in unison.

"Very well then, let's take the cauldrons filled with the boiling mixtures with us through the tunnel and deposit them in the Mystery Mountains, directly into the active volcano at Mount Santiago."

They all flew out of the tunnel. The Dark Wizard spotted them and flew after them, again trying to place spells on them.

"Continue to our destination and wait for me!" Michael Henry called. Then he turned and rammed the wizard at full speed. Before the Dark Wizard knew what was happening, he fell to the ground, unconscious but alive. Magnifying his voice, Michael Henry then said, "I am Michael Henry, the Chosen One, and I wish you no harm. Open the gates of the Crystal City and flee before the battle begins, lest you all perish in the fighting. Master Uror, it is not too late. Surrender immediately! If you do so, neither you nor your troops will be harmed. Just look at the Dark Wizard lying on the ground if you doubt my resolve. This is my first and final warning. You must leave now."

Michael Henry focused on the gates to the Crystal City. As they creaked open, the citizens ran out before Master Uror could react. Michael Henry's voice reverberated throughout the city. "This is Michael Henry, the Chosen One. You must leave the Crystal City now. The gates are open. Do not take anything with you. Leave immediately to save your lives. Do it now!"

Michael Henry called to the Eye of the Tiger and instructed it to go to the Mystery Mountains, saying they would meet at Mount Santiago straightaway. Once at the Mystery Mountains, Michael Henry advised the Eye to warn any creatures living in the vicinity to leave immediately.

Magnifying his voice once more, he said, "This is Michael Henry, the Chosen One. We will be depositing poisonous gasses within the volcano very shortly. All need to exit the area now."

As he landed with the Spirits of the Portal and the cauldrons, he withdrew his yellow crystal. Instantly Princess Marie was there. "Mother, I am about to deposit the gasses into the volcano. Is there anything I need to do?"

Princess Marie said she would contact the hologram of her husband, Prince Knox, to advise them. Several minutes passed, and then Prince Knox appeared to Michael Henry. "You have done well, my son. I am very proud of you. How may I assist you?"

"Father, I believe the best way to dispose of the poisonous gasses from the Dark Wizard is to incinerate the cauldrons inside the volcano. Do you agree?"

Prince Knox suggested that Michael Henry should place a force field around each cauldron that would last for five minutes. Then the spirits should insert the cauldrons directly into the active volcano. Once the force fields wore away, the heat and molten lava should nullify any ill effects of the gasses. However, he also suggested that Michael Henry should monitor the area after the five minutes' time and leave a contingency to verify that the gasses had been destroyed.

"Father, thank you for your guidance." Michael Henry placed the individual force fields and then instructed the spirits to insert the cauldrons in the live volcano, leave immediately, and then return to their landing spot 1,000 yards away.

The spirits did as he instructed, then waited for the five minutes to tick away. Suddenly there was a loud explosion within the volcano, and black fumes spiraled up into the air. Michael Henry knew that all was well. The immense heat in the volcano had done the trick. Confirming there was no trace of gas in the air, he commanded the spirits to follow him to the Dark Portal.

Once at the Dark Portal entrance, Michael Henry reviewed his instructions with the spirits very carefully. "Remember, no one is allowed entrance into the cavern area except for me and anyone who is with me." Then he thought for a moment and added, "King Titus, Queen Coreen, Savannah, Benjamin, and Jonathon should be granted access to the cavern. However, no one except the Chosen One will be allowed to access the portal. These instructions stand until otherwise stated by me, and only by me. The portal has strict orders to this effect, and you must guard against entry by anyone, especially as we draw the net closer around the Dark Wizard and Master Uror. Is that understood?"

They all answered, "Yes, Master."

As they entered the portal, Michael Henry asked for volunteers to be stationed at the Dark Portal. The three spirits Michael Henry had befriended were the first to jump at the chance to serve him. "Very well," he said. "And who will be the first to be stationed at Earth to prevent access from that portal?" Eager to assist, the same three jumped at the chance again.

Michael Henry followed the protocols and opened the portal. He took all twelve spirits with him to Earth and gave further instructions. "Please remember, you must not be seen by anyone—ever! If you are discovered, you could jeopardize our existence on both Earth and the Land of Whoo."

Michael Henry asked the spirits to decide which ones would be assigned to each portal. Initially, he felt they should rotate monthly and provide him with a spirit by his side as needed to go back and communicate with the others about any priorities he might have. Within a few minutes they had reached a decision. One spirit came forward as their spokesman and said the group had elected him to accompany the Chosen One.

Michael Henry nodded his approval. "You will be called Arithmos Number 1, or Arithmos for short." He sealed the cavern again and left through the portal using all the established protocols, leaving three spirits back on Earth.

Next he travelled to the Star Portal, leaving two spirits there, and then back to the Treasure Portal by the Inn of Ethan and left three spirits there. He again journeyed to the Dark Portal, leaving three spirits. He was careful to follow the protocols every time he opened and closed the portals. Michael Henry then left with Arithmos to take the Dark Wizard's canister of poisonous gasses back to the Mystery Mountains and Mount Santiago.

When they arrived at Mount Santiago, Michael Henry again magnified his voice and warned all creatures of his intentions. "Arithmos," he said, "you will need to descend into the live volcano and deposit the canister." He thought this time he would allow ten minutes for his force field to evaporate.

Arithmos was off with the canister and returned with the observation that the volcano had heated up since their last visit. They landed 1,000 yards away to wait the allotted time. Once again there was a burst of black smoke at the ten-minute mark as the force field disappeared. Michael Henry verified that the air was still safe and that the immense heat of the volcano had done its job on the poisonous gasses.

With their mission complete, they flew back from Mount Santiago to the Crystal City. They quickly realized things were deteriorating. Master Uror's troops had managed to close the gates, and the Dark Wizard had started to gain his senses as his troops were preparing to transport him away.

Michael Henry magnified his voice again as he reopened the gates, much faster than before. "Citizens of the Crystal City, this is Michael Henry, the Chosen One, and I wish you no harm. You must flee from the city now to avoid injury. Soldiers of the Dark Wizard and Master Uror, you can see the inevitable is coming. Run away while you can and join your countrymen in the woods."

Michael Henry then blocked the gates open and installed a force field on them to keep them open. Hundreds of citizens and soldiers poured out of the city. Realizing he was again losing control, Master Uror told General Owen to have his best soldiers standing by, ready to move outside the city to prevent citizens from leaving. Already the mercenaries were talking among themselves about deserting Master Uror and running as well.

Michael Henry flew back to the Castle of Providence to meet with his team and check on Savannah. As he landed on the king's balcony, he introduced the new team member, Arithmos Number 1. Then he checked on Savannah to be sure she was okay, apologizing for having to rush off so quickly before. Turning to his team, he advised them about what had happened with the poisonous gasses, explaining how he had been able to destroy the gasses inside the volcano at Mount Santiago with the spirits' help. He then reviewed how he had posted spirits at all portals to prevent any person or creature from entering the Land of Whoo or Earth. He related how he had been visibly shaken to find the canisters being readied for delivery to Earth, targeting the area where he lived outside Marysville, Washington.

"Eye of the Tiger, we need a report on the Crystal City," he said.

"The Crystal City is in disarray. Master Uror's troops are stationed outside the city now, preventing people from entering or leaving. The Dark Wizard has regained consciousness and is back meeting with Master Uror. They believe an attack is imminent and are preparing as best they can."

Michael Henry instructed the Eye to return to the Crystal City and gather information concerning troop strengths and positions. "King Titus, we need archers and the same Special Forces we used in the attack on the Castle of

Providence. Team, can we be ready for an attack by midnight tonight?"

"Yes! Yes! Yes!" They all cheered their agreement.

"Then we are all of one accord! Let's get some rest and meet back here at sunset for dinner. We will start transporting troops and archers as we have done so successfully before."

Jonathon suggested that the Eye of the Tiger should also monitor the woods by the castle to be sure that Master Uror was not planning an offensive before they could strike. Michael Henry agreed and said that when they met again, they would review their plans for the midnight attack.

After everyone had gone, Michael Henry went to Savannah. He wanted to spend some time with his friend to make sure she had not been affected emotionally due to her capture by the Dark Wizard. As they spoke, she related that she was okay and just needed some rest before they all met again at sunset.

Michael Henry really liked Savannah. He wanted to let her know his feelings but realized now was not the time.

CHAPTER 15

ATTACK ON THE CRYSTAL CITY

Michael Henry gathered his team in the king's quarters after dinner and asked for a report from the Eye of the Tiger.

"Michael Henry, there is confusion in the Crystal City. The soldiers of Master Uror and the Dark Wizard have been talking about how both of their leaders hate the other and that no matter what happens, there will be a falling out between the two. Master Uror is questioning the Dark Wizard: How did Savannah slip out of their grasp if she was in a secret *and* sealed cauldron room? What about the spirits who had been working there? What's become of them?

"I have also heard back from my spies. Many of the rodents and snakes have entered the secret cauldron room, along with the bats, and have found no evidence of additional cauldrons or containers of the mixture the spirits were working on. Master Uror found out about the poisonous gasses and is asking for a full report from the Dark Wizard who, of course, has failed to keep Uror up to date, since the wizard had hoped to use the gasses against Uror himself.

"Master Uror was overheard telling General Owen to prepare plans to execute the Dark Wizard, following through on his mandate given earlier, that if the Dark Wizard failed him again, he would pay with his life. There were questions about how to combat the Dark Wizard's spells, and Uror decided to have several archers available with poisonous arrows that could be used when the wizard did not expect it. Master Uror asked that the archers follow the Dark Wizard day and night, waiting for Uror's command, which would be three short blasts from the horn of an ox, followed by one long blast.

"The Dark Wizard also held a conference with his most trusted commander, Skouro, the leader of his troops. This conversation took place in the cauldron room after the wizard unsealed it, resealing it so no one could overhear. Fortunately our rodents were there. The Dark Wizard has conjured up a spell to be placed on Master Uror to ensure his own safety. If the Dark Wizard were to be attacked, wounded, or killed, Skouro will immediately unleash all of his creatures on Master Uror. This distraction would take place just before this spell reached maximum effect, in an effort to keep Master Uror busy and unable to focus on any slight changes in his own demeanor. The spell is basically similar to the ones the wizard used on Queen Alexis and her daughters, only more powerful. This spell will turn the person or creature to stone.

"Skouro asked the Dark Wizard if there was any way he would change his instructions once attacked if he found out the attack had not come from Master Uror. The Dark Wizard replied no. Aware that Michael Henry always seemed to warn any innocents to flee before battle, the wizard felt confident that if he was attacked, it would have to be by Master Uror. He would take other countermeasures against Michael Henry. He told Skouro to implement the plan if he was attacked, wounded or killed."

Michael Henry asked the Eye if there was an undetectable way into the prisons where Jasmine's parents were being held, along with many others. He wanted to use the Medallion to transport them out of the Crystal City.

"Yes," answered the Eye. "If you enter from a cave directly under the Crystal City, there is a tunnel that has not been used in years, having been sealed off once the new tunnel to the prison was completed many years ago. There are no markers in place there to alert the Dark Wizard."

"Very well, my course is clear. I wish to free the oppressed from the prisons before the fighting starts. I will fly there now and transport as many as possible back to the grounds here at the castle. While I am doing this, I need Benjamin, Jonathon, and Savannah to take the sleds and deposit one hundred Special Forces in the woods outside the Crystal City. Savannah, are you feeling well enough to assist us?"

"Yes, I'm much better now and want to help with this mission. Once the troops are in place, I will return and transport a larger number of troops as we did before. Thirty archers are ready for the first pass over the Crystal City."

Michael Henry told Savannah, Benjamin, and Jonathon to start transporting troops as they had discussed so they could again set up a command post to be ready to implement their plans to overthrow the Dark Wizard and Master Uror. Then Michael Henry dove out of the window and headed to the cave that led to the dungeons and prison. Once inside the prison, he gathered all the people together, telling them he was Michael Henry, the Chosen One, and he wished to transport them all immediately to the Castle of New Providence. He told them to gather any belongings and to be certain that all who wanted to leave returned to this spot. He would be transporting from where he now stood.

The captive citizens, including Jasmine's parents, said they were ready for transport. Michael Henry thought to the Medallion, "I wish to transport these people to the courtyard in the Castle of New Providence." With a whoosh, they appeared in the courtyard as Michael Henry magnified his voice and said, "This is Michael Henry, the Chosen One, and I bring back home many of your friends, family, and loved ones from the prisons of the Crystal City. Come now and greet them!"

Then he addressed the group, asking if everyone was okay. They all motioned yes. "I must go back for any others," he said. He leaped up in the air and landed back at the prison, where another large group of prisoners was waiting for transport. Again, with a whoosh, they were back in the courtyard with the others. Many citizens from New Providence had already gathered in anticipation of seeing family members and friends who had been imprisoned for so long. There were many happy reunions as each group was transported from prison to the courtyard while everyone cheered. After each group was transferred, Michael Henry made sure everyone was all right before setting off again to the underground prisons.

This time he arrived at the furthest dungeons and again made his plea to free the oppressed. With one fell swoop, he cleaned out the remaining dungeons and transported the final occupants back to the castle with the others. It was a very thankful group that celebrated as he left again for the Crystal City.

He arrived in the servants' hall, an area where the Dark Wizard had not thought of placing markers. "I am Michael Henry, the Chosen One. If you wish for freedom, you must all come with me now!"

All nodded, waved, and shouted, "Yes, take us with you! Take us with you!" Immediately he transported the entire group, and they were also reunited with their family members.

Once he was sure he had gotten everyone out who wanted to leave, Michael Henry returned to the Castle of Providence to check on troop placements. They were ready for the large force of troops, horses, and equipment to be transported to the area the Special Forces had secured. With one thought, he and the Medallion transported the entire group, including Michael Henry, to the secured area. He checked with his troops and gave his instructions. "Do not attack until we illuminate the grounds in the Crystal City, just as we did during our attack on the Castle of Providence." They all understood what he needed them to do.

Next Michael Henry flew back to supervise as the archers were being loaded. He oversaw their transport to the grounds outside the Crystal City where General Owen's troops were stationed. As they flew over in the invisibility mode, they blanketed the troops with arrows, making one pass after another over their target. The sleds continued to the top stations in the Crystal City and picked off the guards who were on watch.

Michael Henry sent the sleds back for more archers to take their place on the walls. By this time the markers had been set off, alerting the Dark Wizard of their attack. The wizard flew after Michael Henry with a vengeance. However, Michael Henry's reflexes were razor sharp and as quick as a cat, blocking the Dark Wizard's multiple attempts to ram him.

In a bold attempt to stop the Dark Wizard, Michael Henry took off straight up and then made a sharp dive to block the wizard's path, his force field in full protection mode. He hit the Dark Wizard and sent him spiraling a hundred feet before he could recover his flight pattern. Then, with a quick turnaround, Michael Henry again slammed into his enemy, who was busy trying all the spells he knew to try and break through the force field, but with no luck.

Finally the Dark Wizard made a creature call as he commanded every creature to come to his defense. Looking up, Michael Henry saw clouds of condors coming towards him. His first thought was, *This is great!* The archers could get in place, as well as the troops outside the Crystal City, while the Dark Wizard's troops were being distracted by these aerial battles between Michael Henry, the Dark Wizard and the condors.

Michael Henry turned on a dime and headed for the first wave of condors. His tremendous speed caught them off guard and sent them in all directions trying to catch him. He then came to a complete stop, enticing the remaining condors to try and stop him. They all tried to ram him or grasp him in their claws. Of course, with the force field in place, they were unable to claim their prize. The condors ricocheted off the force field, half of them falling to the ground, unable to regain flight, while the other half retreated quickly.

By this time the archers were in place around the Crystal City. Master Uror saw the Dark Wizard's poor showing and decided it was time to blow the ox horn. There was a great deal of confusion on the grounds of the Crystal City as the archers started picking off their human targets.

Michael Henry magnified his voice. "This is Michael Henry, the Chosen One, and I wish you no harm. I will illuminate the grounds so that anyone wishing for freedom may escape. Come to the gates and await my instructions."

Master Uror was ecstatic and told his troops to allow Michael Henry to gather the citizens wishing to leave. Then, as they headed through the gates, General Owen would ambush them as they tried to escape. Even though General Owen's troops had been attacked, they still had strength in their numbers as they waited outside the gates, ready to pounce on the innocent citizens.

Michael Henry gathered the citizens in a group, still unimpeded by the Dark Wizard, and asked if they wished to be transported out of the Crystal City. They all answered yes, and he transported the entire group to the courtyard at the Castle of New Providence. As the people emerged, they rejoiced along with the others in their new freedom from oppression.

Master Uror saw the group vanish and immediately commanded General Owen to search the Crystal City with half of his forces to investigate where the citizens had disappeared to.

Michael Henry magnified his voice again. "This is Michael Henry, the Chosen One, and I wish you no harm. It's not too late to defect if you are a soldier for Master Uror or the Dark Wizard. Run with your hands up, away from this battle site!" With that, while their general was inside the walls with half of his forces, a number of troops outside the walls deserted.

Michael Henry illuminated the grounds and commanded his archers to again blanket the troops with arrows. In the confusion, Master Uror's troops had finally located the Dark Wizard and fired their poisonous arrows at him. He dropped to the ground. With his last words, he began the spell that would turn Master Uror into stone.

Master Uror felt a slight twinge as he overlooked the battlefield and ordered more troops from outside the gates to move inside and support those being pelted with arrows. The Dark Wizard's unswerving commander, Skouro, initiated a creature call, commanding all creatures to attack Uror.

Michael Henry ordered the Special Forces commanders to initiate their attack outside the Crystal City. He again magnified his voice, saying, "This is Michael Henry, the Chosen One, and I wish you no harm. You have no chance for victory over my powers and need to surrender immediately to save your lives. Do it now!" One-fourth of the existing troops did so; those who remained were certainly outnumbered by the forces of King Titus.

General Owen was now in a place of refuge by one of the gates with a small band of loyal troops. They ran to Master Uror, who was hiding until he could escape this onslaught. "Master," the general said, "what are your orders?" There was no reply. General Owen then realized that his trusted warlord Master Uror had fallen under a dark spell of his enemy. Condors dive-bombed Uror, and ten-eyes came at him from every direction. Majors and minors appeared from out of nowhere to assist in the creature call. As Master Uror was overcome by something that seemed to freeze his facial muscles, spreading though his entire body, General Owen remembered the progression of symptoms. "This is the spell the Dark Wizard placed on Queen Alexis and her family years ago," General Owen murmured. He ordered Master Uror be placed on a wagon and he, along with his most trusted troops, managed to escape despite all the fighting.

Skouro found the Dark Wizard paralyzed from the poisonous arrows and immediately called his fleet of condors to transport the wizard to a safer place. Perhaps he could find an antidote to the poison before it was too late.

Michael Henry saw this as his opportunity to gain complete control of the Crystal City without losing any more of his troops in the melee. He first dispatched Arithmos to all the portals, starting with the Dark Portal, to warn the other spirits to be on the lookout for either Master Uror or the Dark Wizard trying to escape from the Land of Whoo. Michael Henry then called to the people, "This is Michael Henry, the Chosen One, and I wish you no harm. I call on both sides to stop fighting." Incredibly, both sides ceased fighting. He went on. "As you can now see, the Dark Wizard and Master Uror have both been eliminated from our city. I declare the Crystal City free of oppression. Soldiers, put down your arms, and you will not be harmed if you leave the city right now. If you wish to swear allegiance to me, you may stay."

When it had all transpired, he spoke again. "This is Michael Henry, the Chosen One, and I wish you no harm. Master Uror and the Dark Wizard have eliminated each other. I will guarantee your safety if you will swear allegiance to me and King Titus. It's time for peace to reign free! Come and join your brothers and sisters who are free in the Land of Whoo."

Amidst all of the confusion, most of the troops relinquished their arms, except for a select group of General

Owen's chosen men who used the confusion to sneak off in the darkness. The citizens of the Crystal City cheered as the remaining soldiers swore allegiance to Michael Henry and King Titus. Michael Henry addressed the citizens, informing them that King Titus would make an appearance soon and that he was also recommending a celebration feast be held within the week to allow for cleanup and proper handling of the stricken citizens and soldiers.

Michael Henry surveyed the damage to the city and thought it best to have his team, along with King Titus and Queen Coreen, make an appearance as soon as possible, but he knew he needed to make a stop first. He flew to the gates of the city and greeted his Special Forces as they entered the city, along with the many archers who had done their best to engage the enemy during this long battle. He showed genuine appreciation for their accomplishments and gave specific examples of their achievements. The archers were excellent shots, and their blankets of arrows had surely saved many lives on Michael Henry's side. The Special Forces had also served well by setting up command posts and securing the area so additional troops could be transported in, allowing them to control the area of conflict. Michael Henry could not have been more pleased with how it had all transpired. Yet something told him it was not over yet.

He flew back with his team to the Castle of Providence and had another debriefing with his entire team, including King Titus and Queen Coreen. He started by thanking all who had participated in the many sorties over the past weeks. Turning to his grandfather and grandmother, he next thanked them for their support and guidance. Then he asked for updates from his team members.

Arithmos related that Skouro had transported the Dark Wizard to the Dark Portal and tried to gain entry, only to find the passage to the cavern blocked by the Spirits of the Portal. Skouro had employed a number of spells trying to break through the force field, but with no apparent luck.

The Eye of the Tiger gave the news that Master Uror's wagon was heading to the Mystery Mountains, guarded by General Owen's troops, and that Master Uror had turned to stone. The Eye also reported that he had been following the Dark Wizard and was aware of the attempt to enter the Dark Portal. When that failed, Skouro had transported the wizard to a site near the Star Portal and was there now.

"Great job, Eye of the Tiger. Keep me posted as usual." Michael Henry then said he had promised the citizens a freedom party during his speech in the Crystal City and that he hoped that King Titus and Queen Coreen could make an appearance. "Of course, you will be protected by a force field from this time forward anytime you leave your quarters at the Castle of New Providence." Turning to Savannah, he asked, "Would it be possible to work with Queen Coreen on the party?" She quickly agreed. "And King Titus, do you agree?"

"Yes," said King Titus. "And while we are at it, let's host a celebration at both the castle and in the city within the week. We will put to work the people you transported here yesterday and ask if they would like to return now as the rebuilding starts on the castle and the city. They can also help us prepare for the celebration. Michael Henry, can you fly over these areas and announce our plans?"

"Yes, of course, as soon as our update is completed."

Benjamin asked how the kingdom would be protected in the coming weeks and months.

Michael Henry had already thought through his answer. "Benjamin and Jonathon, I would like to place you each in charge of a specific location. Benjamin will oversee the Castle of Providence, and Jonathon will be in charge of the Crystal City—if that is all right with you, King Titus."

The king looked proudly at his grandson. "That's a splendid idea, Michael Henry. We shall announce it at each of the celebrations."

"Great," said Michael Henry with a huge smile. "I would like to introduce my team at each celebration individually so the citizens know who helped to free them. Everyone will need to attend, including Cornelius, Eye of the Tiger, Savannah, Arithmos, Benjamin, and Jonathon. Does everyone agree?"

The Eye of the Tiger was the first to respond. "Michael Henry, our continuing defense against traitors and supporters of the Dark Wizard and Master Uror may still depend on our ability to gather information secretly, on a need-to-know basis. Introducing me could hurt us in the long run."

Michael Henry sighed. "Of course you are right. I was getting carried away with our victory." He realized in his zest he had made an error that, if gone undetected, could have threatened the kingdom. He continued, "I agree entirely. And we should probably also exclude Arithmos. The Spirits of the Portals need not be known to our enemies either." Arithmos agreed.

"As a matter of fact," the Eye of the Tiger said, "those still loyal to the Dark Wizard or Master Uror may be at the celebrations. Your presence could gain us additional information as I could listen in on their plans."

"King Titus, how much food will we need?" Michael Henry asked. "Will it be prepared here and then transported to the castle and the city?"

King Titus smiled. "We will have a full staff at both places and plenty of food stores to share. Savannah and Michael Henry, can you fly Queen Coreen over to the castle and the city to inspect what we will need for the celebrations while you make your announcements?"

"Of course," Michael Henry said. "Let's get going. We will have a quick team update when we return in a few hours."

Queen Coreen motioned to Savannah. "Come with me while we tell those in the kitchen what to prepare. Does chicken and pork sound good, along with potatoes and vegetables?" Everyone agreed that it would be fine.

Michael Henry spoke with Benjamin and Jonathon about their upcoming duties. He advised them that they should meet with King Titus to determine how they would communicate with King Titus and Michael Henry. When they had decided this, they could report on it at the next meeting.

By this time, Queen Coreen and Savannah had returned from the kitchen and boarded Cuatro with Michael Henry, who was ready and waiting for them. He gestured for Cornelius to join them and land next to the sled. He did not use the invisibility mode this time; he wanted everyone to see that he was alive and well. He steered the sled to the Crystal City first to check on the cleanup efforts and try to stabilize any areas that might need it. Before he landed, he placed a force field on himself, his passengers, and the sled. As they approached, he magnified his voice. "I am Michael Henry, the Chosen One, and within the week we will celebrate our victory. You will hear from King Titus and meet the people who brought freedom to the Crystal City. Please continue the cleanup efforts, and thank you for your hard work."

They landed in the center of the city. Cornelius agreed to stay by the sled while Queen Coreen, Savannah, and Michael Henry toured the sections being cleaned up, as well as the kitchen facilities and pantries.

Michael Henry addressed the exuberant kitchen staffs, asking for their support for the huge upcoming feast to celebrate the newfound freedom for all the citizens.

When they landed on the king's balcony, Michael Henry found his team gathering for their afternoon meeting. The Eye of the Tiger was the first to speak up, delivering a quick recap of what it had discovered about Master Uror and the Dark Wizard. "General Owen can only make slow progress with the wagon. He is afraid of cracking the petrified figure of Master Uror, so they continue their journey. The Dark Wizard and Skouro have made many attempts to open the portals but with no luck, so they are digging in at the camp they used when the troops were gathering the Treasure of Eagle's Peak. Skouro determined that the cold would slow the Dark Wizard's reaction to this spell and give them more time to find an antidote, if there was one to be found."

"Benjamin and Jonathon, did you reach an understanding about the protocol you wish to use to communicate with King Titus?" asked Michael Henry.

"Yes, we have," Benjamin answered. "We will use the sleds. For the first two weeks, we will return to give King Titus and you updates once a day at noon. Then, if we all agree, we will go to noon every other day for an undetermined amount of time. We will decide together how long it will be. We will also have a system of carrier pigeons available. How does that sound?"

Michael Henry was impressed with their plan. "That sounds great." It felt good to have come so far and have a plan in place for the future of Whoo.

CHAPTER 16

A VICTORY CELEBRATION
- OR NOT?

The time was finally here for the celebration. Michael Henry
met the workers and transported food, utensils, and staff to
the Crystal City as he had advised earlier in the day. Then he
looked around for an area where they could address the
whole city. He located a position that was below Master
Uror's *former* balcony, yet twenty-five feet above ground
level, with enough room for his entire team.

Upon returning to the Castle of New Providence, he
found that the team had already started gathering in the
king's quarters. Michael Henry asked if they would like to be
transported in a group or on sleds. Since his team was more
familiar with sled travel, they all agreed on that option.
Michael Henry took King Titus, Queen Coreen, and
Savannah on his sled, Cuatro. Benjamin and Jonathon took a
second sled, with Cornelius flying alongside. They all landed
in the center of the Crystal City amidst a cheering crowd. As
they waved and greeted the exuberant throngs, the food came
out of the kitchens. Final touches were put in place as the
citizens assembled for the celebration.

Michael Henry led his team up to the small balcony. Magnifying his voice, he said, "I am Michael Henry, the Chosen One. We have all come to help you celebrate your freedom!" The crowd cheered them on. "I want to introduce some of the people who have made this all possible, starting with your sovereign rulers, King Titus and Queen Coreen."

The king and queen stepped forward as the crowd cheered wildly. But as they neared the edge of the balcony, the Eye of the Tiger alerted Michael Henry of an imminent attack. He turned to look towards his grandparents. As King Titus raised his hand to wave to his people, a hooded figure, loyal to Master Uror, commanded his archers to get in position. They aimed their poisonous arrows directly at the king's midsection. The arrows flew through the air but bounced off the activated force fields and fell to the ground. The crowds immediately subdued the archers and the guards took them away.

The king regained his composure and stepped forward with his queen. Titus spoke fondly of the great times in the old kingdom and said that now, with this victory, the new kingdom would be even better. He introduced Savannah and, of course, Michael Henry, and thanked them for their part in achieving the freedom they all now shared.

Then Jonathon and Benjamin came forward to take their bows as the crowds continued to cheer for their heroes. Finally Cornelius was introduced. He let out a giant dragon roar and spewed a twenty-foot flame from his mouth and nostrils.

King Titus thanked his wife and Savannah for arranging dinner for the celebration, and then he invited everyone to partake of the incredible feast set up in the center of the city. He thanked the citizens of the Crystal City and waved as he and the queen, along with the team, prepared to move on to the next celebration at the Castle of Providence. The entire team was cheered as they left on the sleds.

Michael Henry picked out King Titus' old balcony, and the sleds all landed there as they prepared to address the crowds that had begun to gather. King Titus went through the same procedure of introducing everyone, trying not to duck when he saw someone moving quickly. The crowd was very happy indeed to finally see those responsible for their freedom, and they waited excitedly for the festivities to begin. There was charbroiled chicken and pork, potatoes, fresh bread, and plenty to go around for all. As the team joined the citizens of Providence, many came up to King Titus and Michael Henry to tell of their experiences during the battles and how excited they were to finally be free. One man with two small children told how the Dark Wizard had executed his wife, and how much he missed her. But now he knew that his children would have a future without tyranny and be able to live a normal life again.

King Titus told how, before meeting Michael Henry, he had been unsure of his country's survival. But now he knew that Michael Henry would live up to his role as the Chosen One. The more he learned about his grandson, the more elated he was. The king explained how Michael Henry had appeared and taken his place in his army with his hand-picked team, and how he had succeeded in the five trials for the Medallion.

One citizen asked King Titus what the future would hold now that the Dark Wizard and Master Uror had disappeared and were believed to be dead. King Titus responded that he would bring the kingdom together again, and that Benjamin and Jonathon would be in charge of the Castle of New Providence and the Crystal City, reporting back to him on a regular basis to keep both areas secure and peaceful.

"What about Michael Henry? What will he do, King Titus?" asked another.

"I am well pleased with my grandson, and one day he will inherit my kingdom and the Land of Whoo. What do you think about that, Michael Henry?"

Michael Henry blushed as he looked at his good friend Savannah next to him. "King Titus, you are too gracious. Right now my team and I are focused on supporting you and the people and creatures of the Land of Whoo. We wish no malice towards any person or creature in this land. Even though we are still not certain that all elements of the Dark Wizard and Master Uror have been eliminated, we do know both are still missing and presumed dead. My team and I will continue to monitor and research any leads as to their location and situation so that everyone in the Land of Whoo can feel confident as we move forward during the coming weeks. We cannot afford to underestimate them or their supporters. We still have much work to do."

King Titus applauded Michael Henry and his team again. "We all owe you an enormous debt of gratitude, and I am honored to have you as my grandson, Michael Henry."

Citizens kept coming to King Titus and asking questions. "What will you do when you finally locate the Dark Wizard and Master Uror? What will happen to them?"

"I think they should be hanged for crimes against their people!" one citizen said.

King Titus responded that if and when they were found alive, which might not be the case, they would be tried in a court and sentenced based on the laws of the kingdom.

As the conversations continued, Michael Henry was called aside by the Eye of the Tiger. He slipped away from the crowd where he would not be disturbed and the Eye would not be seen as they discussed the Eye's report. "We have not seen any life in the Dark Wizard since he was hit with poisonous arrows," it said. "Skouro was able to get him up in the mountains by the Star Portal and is looking for an antidote as we speak. Master Uror is still cast in stone and has just arrived at their cavern in the desert. General Owen has tried contacting anyone in his command that might have any knowledge about spells, but with no luck at this point."

The Eye turned his attention to what he had learned during the festivities. "During this celebration, several of Uror's supporters discussed how they could overthrow King Titus. They were not aware of the force field until the failed attempt on the king's life in the Crystal City. They considered poisoning your foods and beverages, since the Castle and the Crystal City would be open. They also wanted to know if there were any of the Dark Wizard's poisonous gasses left that could be delivered by condors over the next few days to the Castle of New Providence. It seems they knew of a canister at the Dark Portal and wondered if it could be liberated. Another topic was how they might deliver a weapon to Earth to keep you busy saving that land and away from the Land of Whoo."

As they returned to the balcony, Michael Henry warned King Titus and his team about the possibility of poisoned food or drink in the future. The team stood, waving at the cheering crowd, as they discussed the potential problem. They all decided it would be best to eat together in the king's quarters, just as they had in the past, at the Castle of New Providence. As the discussion continued, Queen Coreen, who had just arrived from meeting with many supporters, suddenly fainted, slumping to the ground. She turned white, and Michael Henry could only assume that evil forces were at work. Not wanting the crowds to realize what was going on, he and the king paid their respects to the cheering multitudes as Jonathon and Benjamin carefully placed Queen Coreen on a cot. Michael Henry transported them all back at one time to the Castle of New Providence, including the sleds.

Once back at the castle, Michael Henry got out his yellow crystal and Princess Marie appeared. He asked his mother about the power of the Medallion to heal the sick, as it appeared that Queen Coreen had been poisoned at the banquet. Princess Marie said that as long as you had no malice towards any person or creature in the Land of Whoo, the best way to use the power was to lay your hand on the person, feeling the power of the Medallion as you thought and affirmed that the person would become perfectly well. Then the ailment, whatever it was, would disappear forever. "I have only used this procedure with one person or creature at a time," Princess Marie admitted, "but I expect that as you grow and mature with the powers of the Medallion, it may be possible with multiple persons or creatures."

Michael Henry bid his mother goodbye and quickly moved to the bedroom where his grandmother was lying. King Titus looked up as he entered the room and related that his wife seemed to have gotten worse once they came back to the Castle of New Providence. He looked intently at his grandson. "Can you help us in any way, using the powers of the Medallion?"

Michael Henry motioned for all but Savannah and King Titus to leave the room. He closed the door, approached his grandmother respectfully, and knelt by her bedside. Reaching his hand to her forehead, he thought, "Medallion, heal my grandmother, Queen Coreen." He could feel the power of the Medallion leaving his hand and going into his grandmother. "Queen Coreen, my queen and my grandmother, you will be cured from your ailment now!"

Both Savannah and King Titus looked at each other and then at Queen Coreen, who opened her eyes, smiled, and then fell asleep. "She is in a weakened state and needs some rest," Michael Henry said quietly. "Let's come back in an hour and check on her condition." King Titus motioned that he wished to stay by the queen's side as Michael Henry and Savannah left the room.

He met with his team right after the incident with his grandmother and reviewed the warnings he had received from the Eye of the Tiger, especially concerning food and drinks, emphasizing that they should all take precautions. As he spoke, the bedroom door opened and in walked King Titus with Queen Coreen, smiling and saying that she was hungry. Everyone cheered and rushed over to talk with her. They could all see she was completely cured.

Michael Henry excused himself and went out to the balcony for a report from the Eye. "We have just left the base where the Dark Wizard was taken by Skouro," the Eye said. "His followers were able to gain access to his quarters today, and in their search they found a small vial that was labeled as an antidote. With us unaware, they have been able to transport it to the Dark Wizard in the mountains and have administered it to him with success. He is up and doing much better but says he needs a day to assess the current situation before heading back. The Dark Wizard did hear that Master Uror had been turned to stone by his spell, and so the wizard added another spell to Master Uror, in addition to the current one. His plans are to fly to Master Uror tomorrow and make certain he never recovers from his current spell."

Michael Henry went back to give his team the news that the Dark Wizard was back and doing better. "I believe we have no choice but to attack him again tonight before he has a chance to regroup his troops and cause turmoil again."

Benjamin was the first one to speak. "Yes, I concur, but we must all remember that it will ultimately be a battle between Michael Henry and the Dark Wizard, just as before."

"I agree," said Michael Henry. "Let's get ready and meet back here in thirty minutes. We will fly the sleds out after him." With that he again consulted the yellow crystal and reviewed the current situation with Princess Marie. She thought it best to contact the hologram of Prince Knox. Within minutes they both appeared to Michael Henry. Prince Knox warned that the Dark Wizard would be very dangerous as he came back from his exile in the mountains and agreed that their plan of attacking tonight would be best. He felt they should renew the force field just before they approached the wizard's hideout. In times past, the Dark Wizard had been able to scan a force field and begin working on a strategy to diminish its effectiveness almost immediately. Prince Knox knew that every time the Medallion updated a force field, it changed slightly, making it more difficult for the Dark Wizard to break.

"Great thoughts, Father," said Michael Henry. Princess Marie gave a parting instruction to have the Medallion verify that the figure they were pursuing was actually the Dark Wizard and not a hologram. "Great stuff, thanks," said Michael Henry, grateful for his parents' help.

He gathered his team, and they prepared to leave for the Dark Wizard's hideout. Cornelius and Arithmos flew alongside the sled carrying Michael Henry, Savannah, Jonathon, and Benjamin. As they approached the snowy mountaintops, he watched their location carefully. Within five miles of the site, Michael Henry landed and advised the Medallion to remove their force fields and to reinstall another of the highest protective nature for each of them. The sled rose immediately, and they continued on to the Dark Wizard's hiding place.

"Medallion," Michael Henry inquired, "do I have the power of reflection, the same as the power of light over darkness?"

"Yes, of course."

"It is possible that the Dark Wizard will try to break our force field and even try various spells on me. When I think 'reflection,' I need you to reflect any spells coming at me back to the Dark Wizard."

"Continue on, Michael Henry. I await your command."

Michael Henry advised his team to stay on the ground at a site a half-mile away from the Dark Wizard. He then magnified his voice and approached. "Dark Wizard, I wish you to surrender. Your life will be spared, and you will be guaranteed a fair trial for your crimes against the people and creatures of the Land of Whoo."

Skouro heard the warning and advised the Dark Wizard to seal off the cavern where he was hiding and wait for Michael Henry to retreat, allowing time for the wizard to regain his strength. But the Dark Wizard would not hear of it and ran out of the cavern. He flew up to meet Michael Henry, and they clashed together above the cold, snow-covered valley. Michael Henry's force field was unmistakably stronger than the Dark Wizard's. After each direct collision between the two enemies, the Dark Wizard fell to the ground, but he bounced right back up to attack once again. Michael Henry was able to turn on a dime and ram the Dark Wizard even as he was still recovering from the last hit. Skouro stood at the entrance of the cavern, trying to send spells skyward against Michael Henry, but to no avail. Nothing seemed to make a connection.

This time the Dark Wizard slowed down, and with a very deliberate motion, he waved his arm toward Michael Henry, casting his most dangerous spell from which there could be no recourse. As Michael Henry saw his arm move, he thought, "Reflection!" and the Medallion immediately reflected the spell back on the Dark Wizard. There was a very loud explosion and the ground below them opened up. The Dark Wizard disappeared into the massive dark hole, screaming, "No…no…no…not this…not now!"

As the ground closed back up there was a strong stench, as if from the rotting flesh of some creature. Michael Henry could not quite figure out what had happened. The Dark Wizard disappeared into this black hole in a flash, and then there was another loud bang that echoed throughout the mountains. Arithmos flew to Michael Henry's side just as the earth closed up over the Dark Wizard. "What was that, Arithmos?"

"Master, your reflection by the Medallion has transferred the Dark Wizard's most dangerous spell back to the Dark Wizard himself. Master, I believe this spell would have transferred you, with your force field intact, into this black hole."

"What was the spell meant to accomplish, besides transferring me into this black hole? I could just be removed by the Medallion back to the surface of Land of Whoo."

"Master, this was no ordinary hole in the ground. This was the entrance to the Underground and is closely guarded by a very powerful field that has never been broken, until the Dark Wizard's gained access through his sorcery. Michael Henry, the Dark Wizard told us he had been experimenting with opening the Underground for years and had just happened upon a breakthrough the month before we were released. Now you have an idea what we lived through and why our desire not to return to this prison of the Spirits of the Underground is so strong."

"Arithmos, could the Dark Wizard do his same spell once inside the Underground to free himself?"

"No, Master. The opening can only be accessed from above ground. If left open, it could release unheard-of plagues that could destroy every living thing in the Land of Whoo."

Michael Henry flew to the Dark Wizard's cavern and looked for Skouro, but he was nowhere to be found. He called for his team to assemble at the entrance to the cavern. The Eye of the Tiger was there in an instant and was the first to enter, looking for anything left behind that could be reused by Skouro. Michael Henry came out after a five-minute search and asked Cornelius to accompany him into the very last portions of the cave. They reentered cautiously and returned with a large stack of black-bound spell books that had been hidden by the Dark Wizard. The Eye was aware of the markers that had been placed in the cave to alert the Wizard if there was any disturbance. "Michael Henry," asked the Eye, "did you see Skouro leave as the attack started?"

"I did not. I did detect a small disturbance in the wall on the outside of this cavern just as the Dark Wizard flew off, but I thought it was caused only by his takeoff."

The Eye went to the site. As the Eye looked for anything unusual, it sensed a presence behind a large rock wall and called Michael Henry over to take a look.

"What is it, Eye of the Tiger?"

"Something is behind this wall." The Eye hovered over the wall, aware of a presence on the other side. "However, their presence can only be felt slightly, and it is diminishing as we speak."

Michael Henry asked his team to step back as he took out the yellow crystal. Princess Marie first congratulated her son for his brilliant idea to reflect the power from the Dark Wizard. Her instructions then were clear. "Use this yellow crystal as you have in the past to remove the wall. Instruct the Medallion to immediately surround the adjacent area with a force field that will not allow Skouro to escape and will also reflect any spells he may try to use back on him before the wall is opened."

"Thank you, Mother," said Michael Henry as her hologram disappeared. He surrounded the immediate area with a force field, and they all removed themselves from the area of the new field. He then shattered the rock wall, which was covering an entrance to a small cave. The Eye of the Tiger could detect the presence of someone inside the cavern. Michael Henry gathered the large stack of spell books and placed them just beyond the opening, moving the force field slightly so he could enter the mouth of the cave. He magnified his voice as he said, "This is Michael Henry, the Chosen One. Come out now and I guarantee you safe passage back to the Castle of New Providence for a fair trial."

Nothing happened. He then gathered some brush, piled it on top of the spell books that were stacked just inside the entrance, and instructed Cornelius to set the whole thing on fire. The mighty dragon gave a loud roar and breathed fire onto the stack of brush. As it burst into flames, Michael Henry and his team gathered more brush to add to the fire. Cornelius continued to breathe fire, and smoke from the blaze soon filled the cave. The Eye of the Tiger signaled that he could sense something or someone getting closer to the entrance. Michael Henry instructed his team to stand back. He checked the force field as the fire burned down slightly, allowing whoever it was to exit safely through a small passage.

Skouro shot out of the cave, almost flying on a dead run for his escape. He immediately hit the force field and was entangled in its powers. He tried spell after spell to escape but with no luck. Michael Henry approached him cautiously and asked if he wished to surrender. Skouro waved his arms at him and Michael Henry spoke the word, "Reflection." The powerful spell broke through the force field, only to be reflected back on Skouro, who crumpled to the ground, writhing in pain. He started to shrivel up until he finally disappeared. The Eye of the Tiger could sense that he was completely gone.

Declaring the cave to be completely clear, Michael Henry commanded, "Let's all return to the Castle of New Providence and tell King Titus of our progress."

CHAPTER 17

RETURN TO NORMALCY

Michael Henry assembled his team back on the balcony of King Titus' quarters at the Castle of New Providence, and approached King Titus with the news. "King Titus, we set out to capture the Dark Wizard to bring him back for trial. He attempted to cast a spell on me that would have imprisoned me for life with the Spirits of the Underground. Fortunately the Medallion was able to reflect this spell back to the Dark Wizard, and he was swallowed up with a loud bang as the ground opened and closed, sealing him forever underground.

"We also tried to capture Skouro so we could bring him back for trial. He too tried to get away, finally casting a number of spells and attacking my force field. With the help of the Medallion, the spells were reflected back onto him. He shriveled up as a result of one of his own spells and disappeared. Finally, before we left, we sealed up the caves they were using, leaving no trace of their existence. I have sent the Eye of the Tiger back to any known quarters of the Dark Wizard and Master Uror to look for any last remnants that could be used against the people and creatures in the Land of Whoo."

King Titus was amazed. "You have been very busy, Michael Henry, and the kingdom appreciates your work and the work of your team. Even Queen Coreen is back to her normal self, thanks to you! And Jasmine, her handmaiden, has been reunited with her parents and is serving her queen as we speak."

Michael Henry opened the group up for discussion before the Eye of the Tiger returned. "What do we need to do next?" he asked.

"On a personal note, my GiGi has been suffering with an incurable disease back on Earth," Savannah said. "When can we get back to give her some relief?"

He gave a heavy sigh. "Yes, I think of GiGi every day as well. Let's first verify that the kingdom is finally secure, and then we can go back to help GiGi. Does that sound okay, Savannah?"

"Yes, but let's not wait too long. I don't want to take any more chances with her life."

Michael Henry wanted to move swiftly too. "I agree. Let's try to wrap up here today and plan on leaving in the morning if nothing else comes up in the kingdom."

Savannah smiled at her friend. "Great."

Jonathon was next, suggesting a safeguard for the Chosen One. "The Medallion has the power to become invisible, so why let everyone know it is hanging from your neck on a chain? If it were invisible, others may not be tempted to steal it." Michael Henry thought that was a great idea and implemented it immediately. Jonathon continued, "There is the power of health over illness. Can the Medallion protect you if you end up eating or drinking something poisonous? The question has not previously been addressed, as far as I can tell."

Michael Henry knew where to go for an answer. He pulled out the yellow crystal and immediately his mother appeared, praising her son and his team for removing the Dark Wizard. "Mother," he asked, "how can I be protected against poisonous food or drink in the future?"

"I am not aware that the Medallion has the capacity to test for poisonous food or drink, but I suspect no one has ever asked for this feature. I know I never did. I wish you well, my son." And with that, she was gone.

Left to his own devices, Michael Henry wondered if it was as easy as simply asking. "Medallion," he thought, "how can I be protected from poisonous food and drink?"

The Medallion communicated to him privately. "Michael Henry, you are indeed the Chosen One, and I do not sense in you any malice toward any person or creature in the Land of Whoo. If you were to be poisoned, you would simply have to decide to get better and it would be so."

Michael Henry conveyed to his team that he had a solution and that they should move on to another question. Benjamin spoke up. "What about Master Uror's stone figure in the Mystery Mountains, hidden by General Owen? Is it possible that he could be rejuvenated the way Queen Alexis was, since it is, in essence, the same spell that was cast on her years ago?"

"Great point, Benjamin. I say let's head out right after our meal and find Master Uror. We can then transport him to the Joshua Gardens and assign Queen Alexis to watch over him. After all, the Dark Wizard did place a final spell on him so he would not be able to come back as Queen Alexis did."

As they started bringing in the food, Michael Henry excused himself to the balcony. "Eye of the Tiger, what have you found?" he asked. The Eye relayed that it had found no information in the last quarters of either the Dark Wizard or Master Uror. "Great," said Michael Henry. "Now, can you go to the hiding place of General Owen and determine our best plan of attack? Then return with the information so we may proceed with the mission."

He entered the room again and enjoyed a relaxing, unrushed meal with his team and the king and queen. Everyone was joking and telling stories about their exploits to either King Titus or Queen Coreen. "King Titus," Michael

Henry said, "how will you protect yourself against evildoers who might want to poison you or someone else on your team, or even Queen Coreen?"

King Titus answered that his kitchen staff consisted of loyal members of one close family. Meals were prepared only by this chosen family, who even tasted them before serving. "Two have thus given their lives to save ours during the time you were away, Michael Henry," the king explained. "Things appear to be quieting down now, but we will continue to rely on this family. They will be the only ones to serve and prepare our meals. We have treated them royally for their sacrifices."

With the meal over, Michael Henry boarded Cuatro, along with Savannah, Jonathon, and Benjamin, and the entire team headed toward the Joshua Gardens to pay a visit to Queen Alexis to ask a favor. The merpeople waved and then alerted the others to come for a meeting. Savannah pointed at the water where she saw Tyler's dolphin guard jumping in the air to alert all the sea creatures of their arrival. The sled hovered inches above the flat waters and waited for Queen Alexis to arrive with her family.

"There they are!" exclaimed Savannah. "I see Princess Kelly and Prince Paul. And look, there's Princess Heather and Prince Benji swimming to join them."

Queen Alexis arrived, shimmering in the crystal clear waters, her crown of jewels catching the sunlight as all her sea creatures bowed before her. "Welcome! Welcome! How can we be of service, Michael Henry? We owe you such a great debt for your kindness and cunning in setting us free from the Dark Wizard and Master Uror."

"Thank you, Queen Alexis, but it is I who owe you for your support in freeing the Castle of Providence. I am here to ask a favor on behalf of the people in the Land of Whoo and King Titus."

"Yes, Michael Henry, what is your request?"

"Queen Alexis, Master Uror has been turned to stone by the Dark Wizard. The wizard added a spell to prevent Master Uror from ever recovering so that he will remain forever encased in stone. We will retrieve this statue, his body, from General Owen and bring it here for safekeeping, if you are in agreement."

"I would be most happy to accommodate your request. I know just the place, deep on the ocean floor where there are creatures loyal to me. They would be most glad to watch over this statue. I also want to tell you that we are planning on the UWL and AWL games returning this year, and we ask that you, King Titus, Queen Coreen, Savannah, and your team all attend the opening ceremonies."

Michael Henry was thrilled at the prospect of being included in the UWL and AWL games. "We would be honored, Queen Alexis! And now I must be off to collect the statue. I will bring it here for you to transport to a place of your choosing."

With the information provided by the Eye of the Tiger, Michael Henry and his team closed in on the hiding place of Master Uror's statue. Michael Henry magnified his voice and called out, "General Owen, this is Michael Henry, the Chosen One. We wish to take the statue of Master Uror to a secure area of our choosing. You and your men will not be harmed if you surrender so that you may be taken to the Castle of New Providence for trial."

General Owen waved the white flag to surrender. Realizing the danger, Michael Henry reinstituted the force field among his team just to be safe. He also thought "reflect" to the Medallion as he entered arrow range of the white flag. Sure enough, twenty-five poisonous arrows whistled through the air. Instantly they were reflected and turned back on the senders. Many of the archers fell in agony as their own poisonous arrows found their marks.

General Owen unleashed a tremendous attack with everything he had. Archers hidden in the rocks outside the entrance released their flaming arrows as catapults fired molten and flaming tar at the team. Of course, Michael Henry reflected all these actions, returning them to their senders as General Owen called his troops to advance and defend their positions.

Michael Henry called out, "General Owen, lay down your arms and surrender. You cannot win against my team. Surrender now and save your life!"

The Eye of the Tiger found Michael Henry and advised him that the stone remains of Master Uror were inside the cave General Owen was defending. Michael Henry asked the Eye to place a marker next to the remains, and he would simply transport the stone statue to Queen Alexis. He left instructions with his team to hold back General Owen's troops until he could return. Then he transported the stone remains of Master Uror to the Joshua Gardens. The Medallion's power held the stone figure just above the water as Queen Alexis and her family swam around it, taking a good look.

"We are honored to assist you and your people by monitoring this once all-powerful warlord, Master Uror," Queen Alexis said. "We have seen the remains of a number of citizens Uror tortured in his chambers and then had executed and thrown into the sea from the Castle of Providence. When we first met Master Uror, we were helping King Titus defend the sea and keep the area around the Castle of Providence secure against anyone who might try to invade. He came across as a military man, someone who had the welfare of King Titus and Queen Coreen at the center of his focus."

"What happened to change your opinion?"

She explained that as Master Uror became more and more powerful, he met a new wizard who convinced him that he should one day rule the Land of Whoo. "This Dark Wizard spent more time with Master Uror as they grew in their greed and power. The kingdom at that time was a happy and secure place. Master Uror and the Dark Wizard formed a deadly alliance that grew secretly as they became more powerful. We had no idea that they had become such allies and had combined so many forces against the kingdom until one day they declared war and started down the road to conquer and enslave the citizens and creatures of the Land of Whoo and the surrounding sea."

She asked him to follow her to transport the remains to a deeper part of the ocean, past the Joshua Gardens. With Queen Alexis leading the way, they approached the chosen spot.

"Let the figure drop here," she said. Michael Henry watched as it descended through the clear waters, disappearing to the ocean floor, never to be seen again by any person or creature in the Land of Whoo.

Queen Alexis looked up towards the sled. "Michael Henry, the people and creatures of the Land of Whoo thank you for giving of yourself to help keep our world safe from aggression. We are eager to continue our partnership. We shall see you again at the upcoming UWL and AWL Games. Thank you again for your commitment."

After bidding Queen Alexis farewell, Michael Henry indicated to the Eye of the Tiger that he had another special assignment for him and that they would need to travel to the Dark Portal. Once outside the portal, he stopped and greeted the Spirits of the Portal. They remained by the entrance as he opened the cavern. His pupils were scanned as he followed the protocols to enter the portal. Michael Henry then informed the Eye of the Tiger that he was sending him to Earth.

"Why so far, Michael Henry?"

"We have not traveled in the portals since the Dark Wizard and Master Uror were eliminated. What if they placed some trap in the portal without our knowledge? Also, I am very concerned about Savannah's grandmother GiGi, who is gravely ill. We plan on going back tomorrow, so I need some recon tonight to be certain it is still safe for us to travel to Earth. As you are aware, the Dark Wizard was about to transport poisonous gasses through the Dark Portal to be used on Earth. As long as we are testing the system, I also need you to travel to the farmhouse and see if everything is okay with Leslie and GiGi. I figure we can complete the surrender of General Owen within four hours. Then I will return to allow you entry back through the portal." He gave the Eye his address to fly by and check on his family as well.

"There is also the possibility that there may be tracking devices on Earth," he went on. "Be on the lookout for any and all suspicious activity, especially the possibility that you may be followed. I will check in with the portal at four-hour increments, having the spirits with me, ready to block any entry that is not warranted. If GiGi is not at the farmhouse, she will probably be in Seattle seeing either Dr. Clark or Dr. Jordan, or with her daughter, Leslie."

He turned his attention to the crystals in front of him. "This is Michael Henry, the Chosen One." He shone his flashlight into the portal marked "Earth," and with a whir, it opened. He sent the Eye of the Tiger for its first portal experience. Then he used all the protocols to close the portal. He had summoned Arithmos to the Dark Portal and had a quick debriefing with the Spirits of the Portal, communicating that they should be on the highest of alerts, as the Dark Wizard could have a spell in place that would have been activated upon his elimination.

Arithmos told his friends how the ground had opened and the Dark Wizard had disappeared into the Underground. They all sighed. They did not wish anyone to experience this imprisonment, not even the Dark Wizard, who had actually imprisoned himself.

Michael Henry flew back to rejoin his team as they negotiated with General Owen, who was still entrenched inside the cavern. Michael Henry magnified his voice and called out, "General Owen, there is no reason for you to persist. I have already transported the remains of Master Uror away to a secure area."

General Owen ran to the back of the cave, only to discover that it was true: Master Uror was gone. There was no reason to continue to hold out.

Michael Henry had landed in front of the cavern with his force field intact, waiting for General Owen to come out. "Medallion," thought Michael Henry, "I have the power of strength over weakness. Do I have superhuman strength as one of my powers?"

"Yes, you do."

General Owen came out of the cave with his sword and armor, running toward Michael Henry. He wanted to fight Michael Henry in hand-to-hand combat. Michael Henry confronted him, saying, "General Owen, you have lost Master Uror. Save your life and surrender now." But General Owen was not ready to give up just yet and swung his fist toward Michael Henry's head. Michael Henry reached out, grabbed his arm, and thrust the general back into the cave. General Owen was not deterred and came out after Michael Henry again, limping on his left side. This time Michael Henry put a force field around him so he could not move.

"I am Michael Henry, the Chosen One, and I wish you no harm," he announced to all who could hear. "General Owen will be taken back to the Castle of New Providence to face trial for his actions against the kingdom. All troops remaining in the cavern, if you come out now, you will be allowed to surrender. You will be transported back to the Castle of New Providence and treated fairly."

With that said, about fifty troops and archers came forward from the cave with their hands in the air. Michael Henry placed a force field around the group as he entered the cave with his team, searching for anything that might be used against them as he illuminated the cave. Finding nothing harmful, Cornelius again doused the cave from back to front with flames just in case they had missed something. Then

Michael Henry sealed the cave with the yellow crystal so no one could discern the opening. With this completed, Michael Henry transported the soldiers and General Owen to the courtyard at the Castle of New Providence and called to King Titus. He and his team bowed down to his grandfather and formally presented General Owen for trial, along with the fifty troops who were in custody.

King Titus raised his hands up and shouted, "This is a great day for the kingdom and all people and creatures in the Land of Whoo! Michael Henry, the citizens and I salute you and your team for bringing peace back to our kingdom on this day. My grandson, in you I am well pleased. From this day forward, this day shall be called Liberation Day in the Land of Whoo. There will be no work on this day, and there will be celebrations throughout the kingdom."

The citizens cheered and in jubilation took Michael Henry and his team on their shoulders, marching around the courtyard shouting, "Liberation Day is here! Long live King Titus and Michael Henry!"

This went on for over an hour. Michael Henry noted the time, knowing he needed to get back to the portal for the Eye of the Tiger. He flew above the crowds, calling down, "Citizens, my team deserves all the credit. Long live the team!" The crowds started the chants and cheers for his team again, allowing Michael Henry to do a few flybys over the crowds and then slip away unnoticed.

He arrived at the Dark Portal and alerted the spirits as he followed all the protocols to open the portal. He stood by, waiting for the Eye of the Tiger to enter. With a whir, the Eye flew through the portal and said, "That was amazing, Michael Henry, but we must talk."

He closed the portal and thanked the spirits for their vigilance as he moved away to a secure area to continue his conversation with the Eye of the Tiger. "Michael Henry, I flew by your house, and it appears that there has not been a very long lapse in Earth time since you left. All is well with your parents. I went to the farmhouse and heard Leslie leaving a message for Savannah on the answering machine. Leslie said she would be there soon to pick her up and take her to see GiGi, who has taken a turn for the worse since you left. Evidently when she was visiting with her new doctor, Dr. Jordan, she had an attack. They rushed her to the hospital and she is stable, but there is not very much time left. I overheard Dr. Jordan asking Leslie to gather the family together tonight as there would only be a few hours left. So I came right back to get you."

Michael Henry and the Eye flew back to the castle and landed on King Titus' balcony. The celebration was still going on in the streets, but the king and the team were back inside. Michael Henry walked over to Savannah.

"Will you come with me to the balcony for a minute so we can talk?" Savannah nodded and went towards the open French doors to the balcony. She didn't like the look on Michael Henry's face.

"Savannah, I sent the Eye of the Tiger back to Earth to make sure the Dark Wizard had not placed any traps in the portal that would activate upon his disappearance. While he was there, he also checked on your family and mine. It appears that GiGi has taken a turn for the worse. Come, we must leave now."

CHAPTER 18

GIGI'S SECRET

After saying their goodbyes, Michael Henry, Savannah, and the Eye of the Tiger rushed to the Star Portal, where they greeted the spirits. Michael Henry followed the protocols to enter, and the portal scanned his pupils as directed. He also directed the portal to communicate with the other portals that he was temporarily leaving the Land of Whoo and that entry from either Earth or the other portals of Whoo would not be allowed. "No one is to enter or leave from Earth or the Land of Whoo except for Michael Henry, the Chosen One. I will be traveling with Savannah and the Eye of the Tiger." He instructed the portal to follow all the protocols he had established.

"Understood, Master," replied the portal. "Your wishes will be communicated as soon as you arrive on Earth. Enjoy your journey."

The portal opened with a whir. Remembering to place the Ring of Aiden and the ring he had received from his grandfather in his pocket, out of sight, Michael Henry joined the others, and the trio entered the opening. They were whisked away to Earth. Michael Henry's and Savannah's bikes were just where they had left them. They jumped on and sped away as fast as they could pedal. As a precaution, the Eye had been rendered invisible by the Medallion to avoid any disturbances on Earth.

As they approached the farmhouse, a car was pulling up in the driveway. It was hard to comprehend that it was the same day as when they'd left, and that only a short time had passed. Savannah dropped her bike, ran to the car to greet her mother and gave her a huge hug. Leslie laughed. "Savannah, you're acting as if I haven't seen you in weeks! It's only been a few hours, honey." She greeted Michael Henry pleasantly and said, "Could you excuse us for a minute while I talk with my daughter?"

"Of course, ma'am." Michael Henry walked over to put his bike against the porch and play with Penny.

Leslie put her arm around Savannah and walked towards the edge of the yard. With tears slowly running down her face, she looked at her only child. "Honey, we need to get to the UW Medical Center to say goodbye to GiGi."

Savannah pulled away. "What do you mean goodbye? When you left you were going to see Dr. Jordan for more tests. What happened?"

"Savannah," said Leslie quietly, "remember, your GiGi has been suffering from a very rare and fatal disease called CJD, or Creutzfeldt-Jakob disease. We knew she had a year or less to live. Sometimes complications can come up, and that is what has happened."

Savannah took a deep breath. "Mom, I would like Michael Henry to come with me to see GiGi. Is that okay?"

"Yes, of course, if it's okay with his parents."

Michael Henry reached in his backpack for his phone and noticed the battery was almost dead. He sent his dad a text. "Savannah's grandmother is sick in the hospital. She wants me to go with them to see her. Is that okay?"

A reply came back. "Yes, it's okay, son. Text me when u r heading home. Dad."

Michael Henry told Savannah it was okay to go with her and they got in the car, Savannah in the front seat and

Michael Henry and the Eye in the back. Michael Henry smiled to himself. If Leslie could see the Eye of the Tiger in her backseat, she would freak out. After what seemed like an eternity, they finally arrived and Leslie parked the car. Her boyfriend, Paul, came walking out of the hospital to meet them, and Savannah introduced him to Michael Henry. Leslie put her arm around Savannah. Turning to Paul she asked, "Can you give us some time together to see GiGi while you and Michael Henry get acquainted?"

"Sure, Leslie. We'll be in the cafeteria. You can text or call if you need us." The boys headed to the cafeteria as Leslie and Savannah walked to the elevators to see GiGi.

The ride up to the ICU was quiet. Once outside GiGi's room, Leslie said, "Don't be disturbed with all the machinery hooked up to GiGi. She has been asking for you, Savannah, so just be yourself and give her all the confidence you can muster."

As they walked in the room, Savannah tried not to gasp. GiGi looked horrible. She had changed so much. How had she become so frail in such a short time? Or was it just her surroundings? Savannah tried to steady her voice. "Hi, GiGi," she said, squeezing her hand slightly.

GiGi opened her eyes and smiled. "Sit down here, child, while we talk for a minute. I need you to be strong for your mother and me. Has she told you about my condition, honey?"

"Yes, of course, GiGi, and I know a miracle will happen and you will be cured."

"Well, child, I would love that, but let's be honest with each other now. Dr. Jordan only gives me a short time, and I am thankful to see you and your mother for as long as I can."

Back in the cafeteria, Paul asked Michael Henry about their day and about his family, trying to open up some conversation. It seemed like no matter what Paul asked, Michael Henry gave an evasive answer. "Are you trying to hide something?" Paul asked finally. "I want to be your friend. What's up?"

Michael Henry took a deep breath. "Well, my birth mother's name was Marie, and my birth father was Knox. They were very much in love when my father died at a young age, fighting for what he believed in. I was adopted by a family, and we just moved into a home not far from Savannah's farmhouse."

"What about your mother? What happened to her?"

"I'm not sure, but I do know she loved me and made many sacrifices for me." With a wisdom beyond his years, he turned the tables on Paul. "So, Paul, what are your intentions toward Savannah and her mother?"

Wow, what a question! "Between you and me, Michael Henry, I would love to have her for my wife. I lost my wife to cancer a few years back and didn't think I would find anyone else as wonderful, but then I found Leslie. Right now she has a lot to deal with, and she needs to put her mother first and foremost. I trust that you will not let Savannah know about our talk. The time is certainly not right for thinking of anything but GiGi's welfare."

"What if GiGi were to somehow receive a miracle cure? What then?"

"Well, that would be a different story. But of course I wouldn't want to rush Leslie until she is ready to proceed with any relationship."

They were finishing their ice cream when Paul got a text from Leslie saying, "GiGi and Savannah are still talking so keep him busy for a bit longer, please."

Paul started talking to Michael Henry about how hard it had been for him growing up with an abusive alcoholic father who would be great during the days, but in the evenings after work could get unbearably out of control. His mother had wanted the best for everyone and was always trying one more thing to save the family. Finally, when Paul went away to college, his parents had several meltdowns and his dad started going to AA. He had been ready to quit at last, and now had been doing well for over ten years. Things were still hard, Paul said, but at least they could talk to each other now.

Paul was doing well in his career, selling virtual servers to large companies, but lately sales had been slow with the downturn in the economy. "What about you, Michael Henry? What do your parents do?"

Michael Henry related how his adoptive parents were absolutely great and hardworking people. His mother had just received a promotion. "She's a nurse, you know, at a dialysis center. She cares for her patients and for her family as well."

Paul's phone vibrated. He looked down and saw a text from Leslie. "Come up to the waiting room when you can, please." He picked up the tray and said, "Looks like we've been summoned. Let's head up to the waiting room to give the girls all the support we can. I have enjoyed our short visit, Michael Henry, and I know I can count on you to keep our discussions in confidence."

"Of course, Paul. No problem."

Up on the ward, Paul and Michael Henry arrived just as Leslie and Savannah were coming out of GiGi's room. Leslie's eyes were red as she walked towards Paul. "We've talked with Mom, and she is at peace with whatever the outcome will be."

Savannah looked over at Michael Henry, and they exchanged a knowing glance. They saw a doctor coming down the hallway. Dr. Jordon stopped to greet Leslie, and she introduced him to Savannah and Michael Henry.

"Hi, I'm Dr. Jordan. I am here to follow up on GiGi. Give me a minute with her and then we can all talk for a few moments, if you would like." He shook hands with Savannah and Michael Henry before heading into GiGi's room.

Savannah motioned to Michael Henry and they walked down the hallway. She told him about GiGi and how the disease, CJD, was very rare. She could tell it was taking its toll on GiGi, and she could see her strength disappearing. GiGi had also mentioned that the doctor seemed to be a bit more distracted as the day progressed. "When can you be alone with GiGi so you can help her regain her health?" Savannah asked. She said she would make an excuse for the both of them to talk with GiGi privately so they would not alert the others to Michael Henry's powers.

Dr. Jordan came out of GiGi's room, long-faced. He visited first with Leslie. He told her that tonight would most likely be the last night GiGi would be with them and that they should do all they could to comfort her. He asked if it was all right to speak freely in front of Michael Henry, and Leslie gave the okay to proceed. Dr. Jordan looked at those gathered outside GiGi's room. He seemed to take a deep breath and then proceeded to tell them a bit more about the disease and how its consequences were always lethal. He concluded by reaffirming that there was nothing further medicine could do.

Leslie thanked Dr. Jordan for his concerns but then asked if he was all right, that it looked like something was bothering him. "Well, Leslie," Dr. Jordan confessed, "my son Zack and a friend are on a climbing expedition this week on Mount Hood. I had expected to hear from them today. They are both very experienced climbers, but I still worry about them."

They all visited for another minute, and then Dr. Jordan left to check on his son. Michael Henry walked down the hallway and around the corner. He stopped out of sight of everyone while he conversed with the Eye of the Tiger. "Do a flyby of Mount Hood, searching for any climbers who may be stuck around the top, and then let me know what you find," Michael Henry instructed. He had barely finished speaking before the Eye was off.

He walked back down the hallway towards GiGi's room and heard Leslie talking with Savannah. Paul was standing by to give the family all the support he could. After a long interlude, Savannah asked if she could talk with GiGi alone.

"Of course, honey," said Leslie. "Are you sure you don't want me to come with you?"

"No, Mom, I need to face this by myself. And after I talk with GiGi, I will call Michael Henry into the room, and then everyone else after that. Is that okay with everybody?"

"Yes, of course, if that's what you want. Are you sure?"

Savannah nodded and went back into GiGi's room. "GiGi," she started slowly, "I want you to listen carefully. I am here to give you a miracle. You cannot reveal this miracle to anyone, and I need you to promise not to tell."

GiGi looked at her only grandchild. "Honey, don't talk in fantasies. I know my hours are numbered, and I want you to know and understand what this really means."

"Very well, GiGi. Just promise me that when you are cured you will not reveal the source to anyone, not even my mom or Paul."

GiGi smiled. "Honey, I certainly want to live and watch you grow up. If it will make you feel better, I promise, and I am ready for anything you may have to offer."

Savannah opened the door and waved Michael Henry in. As he entered, she asked if he could truly help GiGi achieve health over illness. He smiled at his friend and closed the door. Then he looked over at GiGi. Because of all of the machines, no one could see much through the window in the door. There were only machines and their built-in alarms to keep the three of them company.

"GiGi," said Michael Henry quietly, "I am the Chosen One. As I sit next to you, I will lay my hands on your forehead. Savannah, I need you to be in line with me and the window so no passersby are able to see what we are doing."

Just then, there was a knock on the door. A nurse and Dr. Jordan entered the room. They looked at the data on the machines and at GiGi's chart on the computer monitor, and then asked if Michael Henry and Savannah could step out for a minute so they could check GiGi and give some medicine through her IV to soothe her for the night. Michael Henry and Savannah stepped out of the room and found Paul and Leslie over by the windows. Dr. Jordan came over to talk with them again a few minutes later. He said there wasn't much change, but that he had given her something to help make her more comfortable.

Leslie asked if he had heard from his son. He said he had not, but that in the morning he was going to charter a helicopter and start his personal search for his son. He would check on GiGi before he left. He reiterated that there was really no change, that GiGi's vital signs were actually slipping and that they should be prepared for the worst.

As he walked away, Savannah and Michael Henry reentered the room. Savannah stood in the line of sight from the window to Michael Henry, who was already seated next to GiGi on the bed. As he laid his hand on her forehead, GiGi smiled at him. He spoke with quiet confidence.

"I am Michael Henry, the Chosen One. I have no malice toward any person or creature in the Land of Whoo, and I certify that the same is true on Earth. GiGi, you will be fully healed of any ailments and be one hundred percent cured as of—now." As the words came out of his mouth, he could feel power leave his hand and go into GiGi as she smiled back at him. "GiGi, it has been my experience that you will be very sleepy. But when you awake, you will be able to rise from your bed, and your health will be restored."

GiGi did seem very sleepy as Savannah called Leslie and Paul into the room. Leslie looked at her mother and said, "Let's all let her rest a bit." They went out into the waiting room and tried to talk, but no one knew what to say. Michael Henry excused himself and again walked down the hallway. He could sense the return of the Eye of the Tiger.

"You're back," he said. "Give me an update, please."

"Well, Michael Henry, after several sweeps, I have located the climbers. It is dark in their location. Zack, who is Dr. Jordan's son, cannot move his legs, and his friend Aaron is stuck under a boulder. They have both lost a lot of blood. I have my doubts whether they can make it through the night."

"Eye of the Tiger, stand by and we will travel to the climbers in a few minutes." With that, he walked back to the family as some nurses went into GiGi's room.

One of the nurses said to Leslie. "Why don't you go to the cafeteria? We will come and get you if anything changes. GiGi is resting comfortably now."

Michael Henry called Savannah over to the side and told her what he had learned about Dr. Jordan's son, Zack, and that he may not make it through the night. "I'm going with the Eye of the Tiger to see what I can do. Can you cover for me while I am gone? Just say I was very concerned when I saw GiGi, that I needed to go for a walk and be by myself for a while and said I would text you shortly."

Once in a secluded spot, he took off with the Eye for Mount Hood. Soon he landed next to the trapped climbers. With his great strength, he lifted the boulder off of Aaron, who was in shock. Then he looked at Zack, who was also caught under some boulders. Michael Henry asked him if he could move his legs. Zack shook his head no. It appeared that he was paralyzed from the waist down.

"All right, guys, it looks like you will be just fine," Michael Henry said. He could see that they were going in and out of consciousness. He placed his hand on Zack's forehead. "I am Michael Henry, the Chosen One. I have no malice against any person or creature in the Land of Whoo, and I certify the same to be true of Earth." He felt a power travel through his hand to Zack's forehead as he said, "You will be fully cured of any ailments as of now." Without waiting, he did the same for Aaron, feeling another power surge leave his hand and go into Aaron's forehead.

Once Michael Henry could tell the boys were stable, he transported them in the invisible mode to the helipad by Graves Field. He noticed a climber's personal locator beacon that had not been activated in their gear. They must have been pinned so suddenly that they couldn't move to set off the device. Michael Henry left the boys on the helipad, activated the PLB, and transported himself back to the hospital.

It wasn't long before Dr. Jordan received a call from the PLB monitoring service since he was the primary contact for Zack's device. "Where is my son?" he asked frantically.

The monitoring company had triangulated the area. "He appears to be at the Graves Field helipad."

"He must be at the heliport and somehow activated the alarm. But why would the rescue copter just leave? No matter." He slammed the phone down and rushed to meet the ambulance at the ER entrance.

Dr. Jordan was with Zack as he went in and out of consciousness. All he could think of was his son's welfare and whether he was truly going to be all right. The ER doctor, Dr. Larry, was already running tests and would have some news very shortly. Dr. Jordan sat by his son's bed, waiting.

After a short while, Dr. Larry called him out of the room to look at the tests. Both doctors were astonished at the results. "He appears to be perfectly healthy and unharmed!" Dr. Larry exclaimed. He had asked Zack if he could move his leg and, to his amazement, he could. The results for Aaron were equally as baffling. How could the tests be normal given their outward appearance?

"It's too soon to make any decisions," Dr. Larry reminded his colleague. "We have more tests to do. But their vitals and movements appear to be normal."

Michael Henry walked into the cafeteria just as the family was going back up to see GiGi. They had gotten a message from the nurse to return quickly. He caught up with

Savannah as they got on the elevator and went back to the room with them. When they arrived, GiGi was awake and sitting up, trying to get out of bed, saying she wanted to go home. The nurse told them she had a call in to Dr. Jordan, who was in the ER with his son, Zack.

The family gathered around GiGi, who appeared to be in fine health, smiling and hugging her daughter and granddaughter. The nurses asked that they take it easy and wait for Dr. Jordan to arrive before they tried to help GiGi out of bed. It seemed like an eternity, but Dr. Jordan finally entered the room. He immediately asked to be alone with GiGi and the nurses and could be seen shaking his head in disbelief.

He came out of the room smiling. "GiGi seems to be doing better, but let's not get ahead of ourselves. Her vital signs are good and she is stable. I would recommend that you all go home and get a good night's rest, and let GiGi rest also. In the morning we can run additional tests, and by noon, we should have some answers. With GiGi's improvements tonight, we feel that she will be fine until the morning."

Leslie asked Dr. Jordan if his son was okay. "Absolutely! He showed up on the helipad a short while ago."

"How was he rescued?"

Dr. Jordan was still wondering that himself. "His PLB went off. I assume a ranger's helicopter was in the process of dropping him off and possibly got another call. It's all very peculiar. But the most important thing is that he is here in the ER, along with his friend Aaron. We will get more information after some tests are run later tonight and in the morning. All I really know is that he is all right. Maybe because I work here the rescue team thought I should meet Zack and they got another call. I just don't know."

Now Paul was curious. "What does Zack say about it, Dr. Jordan?"

"Who knows? He said he had been going in and out of consciousness, but his thoughts seem to be very mixed up. He said he was trapped and could not move his legs. Then someone showed up to help him, and the next thing he remembers is being dropped off on the helipad. He keeps saying he was paralyzed and that this person healed him. It sounds to me like he was delirious.

"It looks like we will all get some rest tonight and be back in the morning to continue tests on our loved ones. Why don't you head home?"

Leslie nodded. "Michael Henry, how about I give you a ride home, and we can call you in the morning?"

"Sounds great," said Michael Henry.

Dr. Jordan went back to the ER to check on his son. Both boys were completing more tests, and the results showed the same as the earlier tests—everything was normal. Aaron's wife had just arrived and was shown to his room. The night would give them all a chance to rest, and they could sort everything out in the morning.

CHAPTER 19

THE MYSTERY DONOR

Dr. Spencer Jordan arrived early to make his rounds. He saw that GiGi was up and alert and asking to be released. "Settle down," he said, "let's continue running tests. I will be back in a few hours." He had already checked on Zack; he and Aaron were still asleep, so he wanted to let them get some additional rest.

Dr. Jordan went by the ER to get some information on the chopper that had brought Zack in the night before. He wanted to personally thank the team and find out about the successful rescue. To his amazement, no one had any report of the chopper. He asked his friend Blain, who was in charge of security at Airlift Northwest, if he could see the tape from the night before. Blain had told him no problem, to just drop by the security office by the helipad. He would be there for about an hour.

Blain had already keyed up the helipad CCTV camera and waited for his friend Spencer to arrive. He checked the security log from the night before and saw a call recorded at 10:02 from a pilot leaving to pick up a victim of a car accident. He set the search mode for 9:55 and began.

Dr. Jordan knocked on the door to Blain's office. "Is this some kind of a joke?" Blain asked.

"No joke. Let's look at the CCTV and I'll tell you all I know."

"Fair enough." They sat in front of the monitors as Blain looked at the search mode for the helipad camera. They stared at the screen but there was nothing to see. Then all of a sudden, at 10:01, the boys appeared on the helipad as an Agusta 109A helicopter was lifting off. According to Blain's log, the pilot had radioed at 10:02 that he noted a strobe light after liftoff.

"Spencer, how did you know they were at the helipad?" Blain asked.

"I gave Zack an ACR 406 Personal Locator Beacon that is part of the COSPAS-SARSAT system and had it registered to call my cell phone in any emergency. It's a small unit that can be carried in your pocket or pack, and once activated, is accurate anywhere in the world to one hundred meters. This particular unit has a very bright LED strobe light. When the system called me, they gave the location as the UW helipad near Graves Field. I just assumed it was accidentally set off by the rescue helicopter."

Just then Dr. Jordan got a call on his pager that Zack was up and asking for him. He excused himself, and Blain said he would continue checking.

Back in Zack's room, Dr. Jordan looked at the computer screen and saw his son was completely normal, according to his chart. Zack was sitting up in bed, saying, "Dad, get me out of here, would you?"

"There are still a few questions we need to get sorted out, and I want to walk over to Aaron's room and see his parents. Tell me what happened, son."

"Well, we were climbing the Sandy Glacier Headwall Route, like we told you before we left. Remember, it's in that remote area of the northwest face on the Oregon side of Mount Hood. There was a rock slide, and we slid down partially into a crevice. It happened so fast I couldn't stop myself. I remember talking to Aaron, who had slid down next to me. I was trapped and couldn't move, and so was he. We lost a lot of blood and were going into shock. I vaguely remember someone showing up, like in a fairy tale. I thought he pulled us both out from under the rocks. The next thing I knew, we were at the helipad. I thought I must have been delirious because it didn't make sense."

"Okay, son, take it easy here for a while. Let me go next door and see Aaron and his parents."

As Dr. Jordan entered the room, Aaron's mother, Janet, immediately approached him. "What has happened to our sons?" she asked.

"What do you mean?"

"Aaron tells me he doesn't remember much about his climbing accident. I called Portland Mountain Rescue and the sheriff's department, and there are no reports of any rescue operations yesterday. So tell me, how did they get to the hospital, and how did you hear about their accident?"

Dr. Jordan recapped what had happened and said they were still checking into it, but that he could not figure out how their PLB had been activated, or who had activated it.

Janet asked how Zack was and said that she was so sorry to hear of his paralysis. "Aaron said Zack talked to him while they were trapped. Zack said he couldn't feel anything from the waist down."

"He's not paralyzed," Dr. Jordan said in wonder. "He's perfectly fine."

Down in GiGi's room, the family had arrived, and GiGi was ready to go home. The nurse paged Dr. Jordan to the room. Leslie and Paul were talking with GiGi just like before she'd become sick.

Dr. Jordan arrived and looked at GiGi's charts again, still in disbelief. Earlier he had called her original physician, Dr. Clark, who was also there reviewing the tests. They both told the family that all the tests indicated that GiGi had been completely cured of this very rare and incurable disease. They said they would love to continue testing her to see if they could find something that could possibly help others who had CJD.

Dr. Jordan asked GiGi when she'd started feeling better. GiGi just looked at Savannah and smiled.

"Did Savannah do something that caused these remarkable results, GiGi?" Dr. Clark asked.

GiGi smiled again. "Dr. Clark, you did a wonderful job, and I was fully prepared for the inevitable. Now I am fully prepared to live the rest of my life with my family and enjoy it to the fullest, every minute of it."

After conferring, both doctors agreed that GiGi was free to go home. They said she appeared to be better than before she'd become ill in the first place.

Leslie cried as she helped GiGi get ready to leave. "What do you want to do this afternoon to celebrate, GiGi?"

GiGi said she would just like to go home to the farmhouse and cook a big meal for her family—"and oh, yes, let's invite Michael Henry to join us."

Dr. Jordan told Dr. Clark how his son had wound up on the helipad and was also in great shape. Dr. Clark wondered if there was anything in common that could have helped GiGi, Zack and Aaron.

"Three miracles in the same hospital at roughly the same time? Someone's guardian angel must have been working overtime," said Dr. Jordan with a laugh.

Soon he signed the release papers for GiGi. He wished the family well and said he would like to call GiGi sometime in the future. He would schedule an appointment with her in thirty days at his office for a follow-up visit. If she could remember anything that might have caused her cure, he would appreciate any feedback.

Zack was also feeling great, and there was no reason to keep him in the hospital. He and Aaron were also being released that morning. Zack said he thought he'd seen a young man appear to him on the mountain, and that he'd helped free him and Aaron with superhuman strength. Then he'd healed them, and the next thing he was aware of, they were at the helipad. "Sounds weird, Dad, but that's all I know," he said.

Dr. Jordan had been trying to figure out what had happened. He knew it was possible for Zack not to remember something accurately while he was on the mountain. But how had they both just appeared at the helipad with no helicopter? Was there a problem with the camera system? Had they been dropped off by a rescue chopper? But if that was the case, why would the chopper not stay or even call in, as was their protocol?

Whatever had happened, Dr. Jordan knew he wouldn't find an answer any time soon. He wondered if it could be tied to GiGi's strange cure. Whatever it was it was, and he was grateful for his son's return.

Back at the farmhouse, GiGi was cooking a delicious meal for her family. Michael Henry rode his bike over to visit with Savannah and see how GiGi was doing. GiGi called him and Savannah into the kitchen.

"When can we talk about what happened?" she asked.

"Anytime, GiGi," said Michael Henry.

"Okay, let's wander down to the pond for a few minutes so no one will bother us." They walked outside together. When they were out of earshot of the house, GiGi said, "Michael Henry, you saved my life, and yet you do not want the credit. I want to tell everyone what happened. How did you just walk in and do what you did?"

"Well, GiGi, as we discussed earlier, I could give you a complete cure, but you could not tell anyone what happened. Maybe one day, but not now."

"I do know that Savannah was very confident that you could perform a complete cure of my illness. Why would she feel that way?"

"GiGi, as you know, Savannah is a very special person and friend, and I know she loves you very much. She risked her life to save yours. She was very supportive of me when I was pursued by a number of evil entities in faraway places, and she has always loved and believed in you and her family. I still must ask for your silence, and I need your assurance that you will honor our agreement."

"Of course, Michael Henry. I know you saved my life and that Savannah was part of my cure as well, so I will honor your wishes. I will be going over my medical bills in the next week or so. Before I was counting on the death benefit on my insurance to help cover my expenses; now, of course, I will need to find a way to get by but I'll figure that out later. I will keep your power a secret and not say anything of your adventures, whatever they may be."

"Great. Savannah, let's take our bikes for a ride on the trail before dinner and let GiGi visit with Leslie and Paul. I have an idea." They took off, along with the Eye of the Tiger, and rode to the portal for a quick trip before dinner. They entered the cavern and Michael Henry opened the portal. With a whir, the three were whisked away.

"Let's give GiGi a welcome home gift that will pay for her medical bills," he said. He took Cuatro to Grace Island where the treasure was hidden. He waited for the tide to be right to enter, and then the pair went in and picked out a handful of diamonds and emeralds, along with two small gold bars and put them in his backpack. Michael Henry had sent the Eye of the Tiger for a quick report while they searched the treasure. The Eye returned to say all seemed to be quiet in the Land of Whoo.

Michael Henry, Savannah, and the Eye of the Tiger returned to Earth and closed the portal. They rode back to the farmhouse, and GiGi came down to the pond to greet them, along with Penny. They walked back to the farmhouse together, with GiGi in great spirits.

The family sat down to a marvelous meal that was very much like Thanksgiving dinner with turkey, GiGi's special dressing, sweet potatoes, topped off with homemade strawberry and cherry pies for dessert. GiGi said she was very thankful for all the blessings she had received, that last Thanksgiving she had not felt like giving thanks but that had all changed. She said how thankful she was for her family and friends, including Michael Henry.

After dinner Paul walked with Leslie down to the pond and told her that he would like their relationship to get more serious, now that GiGi was better.

"Let's not rush into anything," Leslie said, "but I agree." She was looking forward to a stronger relationship with Paul.

Michael Henry asked the Eye of the Tiger to check on Zack and Aaron and get back with him in the morning.

The family at the farmhouse was very happy. Savannah rode her bike with Michael Henry out to the road and asked him to come back the next day.

"See you tomorrow." He turned and rode down the lonely road toward home. His family was there when he arrived. He told them about the great turkey dinner and how GiGi had recovered. They talked for a few minutes and all was well. Sam talked about her new job duties and how she was doing, and Dan said his roofing job was still going well. They asked Michael Henry about his day, and he told them how happy GiGi and her family were now that she had a clean bill of health.

The next morning the Eye of the Tiger reported that Zack and Aaron were doing well, that they were still a bit fuzzy about what had happened, and their parents were still very curious. The young men were driving out to Mt. Hood that day to retrieve the car they'd left behind for their climb, so all was well.

"Eye of the Tiger, find me a reputable jeweler who will buy my diamonds and not reveal the source. Then fly by the UW Medical Center and get the amount of GiGi's bill." The Eye was gone briefly and then returned to report that there was a jeweler in Marysville advertising cash for gold jewelry and precious stones. He also communicated that he was able to retrieve GiGi's account information.

Michael Henry pulled the yellow crystal from his backpack and Princess Marie appeared. "I am very pleased with how you have implemented the power of the Medallion," she said. "How may I help you, son?"

"Mother, I would like to help GiGi pay for her medical bills, but I wish to do so anonymously."

"Let's go to the jeweler's office, and I can do the talking to pay for the medical bills."

"Great." He and the Eye of the Tiger used the invisibility mode to hide their identity as they were transported to the jeweler's office. When the jeweler, Mr. Ramsey, was alone, Michael Henry entered his office. Using the yellow crystal, he called Princess Marie, who appeared as he placed the jewels and the gold bars on Mr. Ramsey's desk. She asked him for an estimate on the items in front of him.

"Where did you get these diamonds?" he asked. "They are of the highest quality." He gave her a fair estimate. Princess Marie told him to apply the full amount to GiGi's medical expenses, along with the explanation that the gold and diamonds had been in the family for generations. She asked that the money be paid anonymously to the UW Medical Center and gave him the account information. She also told Mr. Ramsey to apply his usual service fee to the transaction and said that if there were any funds left, he should go ahead and apply them to GiGi's account.

With her long raincoat and a scarf covering most of her face and hair, Princess Marie seemed to fit in with the many other hurried Marysville customers. She asked for a receipt for the items Mr. Ramsey had received, along with a letter stating that he would disburse the funds within twenty-four hours.

"Great, then my business here is finished once you give me the letter," she said. Mr. Ramsey left and soon returned with the letter he had signed. Princess Marie smiled.

"I know I can trust you to deliver these funds anonymously, Mr. Ramsey, within the twenty-four-hour period we agreed upon. Let me assure you that I have the means to follow up if you should fail to complete our agreement on time."

"How so?"

Princess Marie had already gained access to Mr. Ramsey's bank account information from the Eye of the Tiger. She now turned towards a wall and a hologram appeared, showing Mr. Ramsey's personal information, including an up-to-the-minute banking report and his 401k plan. "I know I can trust you, Mr. Ramsey. Thank you again for your services," she said, leaving as quickly as she had arrived.

Mr. Ramsey shook his head in amazement. He knew that she meant business. He processed the payment immediately.

Michael Henry thanked his mother and headed home, where he got on his bike and rode to GiGi's house to see what might have happened since he'd left. "At the front gate," he texted Savannah.

"Be right there," she texted back. She arrived on her bike and the two pedaled back to the farmhouse, talking as they rode down the long driveway. Michael Henry told Savannah how much he missed his grandparents. They both agreed that a trip to Whoo was a great idea and decided to go the next day. As they entered the yard, they saw GiGi on the porch, just getting off the phone. As she walked down the steps to meet them, she seemed very excited.

"You are the first people to hear this great news," GiGi said.

"What's that?" Savannah asked.

"Well, honey, the UW Medical Center just called me about the monster bill I incurred over the past year. It turns out that someone anonymously paid the bill in full this afternoon. Michael Henry, I have to wonder if you are

206

somehow as responsible for my good fortune as you were for my recovery."

"GiGi, your family needs you, and you deserve to be happy without the great debt burden from your illness. Whoever helped you out was certainly a friend of the family."

GiGi gave him a giant hug, and he blushed as they walked up the steps, arm in arm, into the farmhouse so she could tell Leslie and Paul of her good fortune.

CHAPTER 20

THE ANNOUNCEMENT

King Titus and Queen Coreen were planning the next grand ball for all citizens, and the king was now looking to return the lands of Whoo to their rightful owners or their descendants.

In a surprise ceremony, King Titus had invited all the citizens to gather at noon at the Castle of New Providence. There he crowned his grandson Prince Michael Henry from his balcony, where all the citizens could clearly see Michael Henry being rewarded for his efforts. He gave the land and property of Count Aiden to his grandson. Next he crowned Benjamin and Jonathon as administrators of the Crystal City and the Castle of Providence, reporting directly to King Titus. Then King Titus and Queen Coreen gave a special crown to Savannah, and she was crowned countess and given lands and a house next to Michael Henry's.

"Attention...attention!" King Titus cried. "Citizens, I, King Titus, ruler over the Land of Whoo, formally announce that Michael Henry is indeed my grandson and from this day forward shall be called Prince Michael Henry. He will someday inherit the throne and the kingdom of Whoo. He is young and powerful and has many good deeds to complete before he is ready to settle down in any one place."

The king asked him to address the crowds. Michael Henry and Savannah walked to the edge of the balcony as the crowds chanted, "Long live Prince Michael Henry and Countess Savannah!"

Michael Henry gave his grandfather and grandmother a hug as the crowd continued their chanting. With Savannah by his side, he addressed the crowds. "I want to take this opportunity to thank my team. As I call your name, please step forward. First is Savannah, who was captured by the Dark Wizard and fought by my side the entire time. Next let me introduce Benjamin, who is my military advisor, and Jonathon who gave up years of his life to be the messenger for the Medallion. Without his assistance, I would not be standing here today. Then Cornelius—we could not have won our battles without him. He is our dragon!"

The crowds were wild with excitement for Michael Henry and his team. Then the prince said, "I must also take a solemn moment to thank those who are no longer with us, and dedicate a moment of silence to their memories. My mother, Princess Marie, who continues to lead me with her wisdom, and my father, Prince Knox, who also sacrificed his life so many of us could have this day."

King Titus stepped up to the balcony and said, "From this day forward, today will be remembered as Memorial Day in honor of my fallen comrades, like my good friend, Count Aiden; my son, Prince Knox; my daughter-in-law, Princess Marie; and the many others who sacrificed so much so that we could return to peace and prosperity, free of the oppression of the Dark Wizard and Master Uror. Spread the word that on this day there will be no work for anyone, including my staff. Everyone will enjoy a holiday to formally celebrate Memorial Day in the Land of Whoo."

King Titus hosted a brief lunch for the prince's team and then let his staff off for the rest of the day to enjoy the celebrations at the Castle of New Providence. Then he, Queen Coreen, and Michael Henry's team boarded two sleds and flew to the Castle of Providence and the Crystal City to repeat the coronation and officially announce that that day would henceforth be known as Memorial Day.

The sleds headed back to the Castle of New Providence, and Michael Henry consulted again with the Eye of the Tiger, who said all was well. The prince asked King Titus if he would ever move back to the Castle of Providence, where he had lived before the wars began.

"Maybe someday," the king answered, "but my focus now is uniting our three territories; addressing any peacetime issues to make our lands stronger; and promoting peace, prosperity, and stability in the Land of Whoo." He went on to say that he was looking forward to having the creatures of Whoo help with farming the land. He saw no reason why the kingdom could not use more modern techniques to plant their fields, sow their crops, and effectively use teams for harvesting. That was going to be the king's project while Jonathon and Benjamin helped administer their respective areas.

Michael Henry had already discussed returning to Earth with both King Titus and Queen Coreen. They clearly understood the need to be present in both worlds as things settled down. He, Savannah, and the Eye of the Tiger made their trek to the Star Portal on Cuatro. The prince greeted the Spirits of the Portal and told them he appreciated their very necessary work. He followed all the protocols and the portal opened with a whirring noise and lights as they entered and headed back to Earth.

The portal opened on Earth to allow them passage, and Michael Henry again thanked the spirits on the Earth side for a job well done. He sealed the portal and instructed that there should be no entry from Earth or the Land of Whoo except by him alone.

"Yes, Master," the portal replied. "What is your direction regarding the other portals that are open in this cavern on Earth, housing the portal to the Land of Whoo?"

Michael Henry illuminated the other portals with his flashlight and asked if there had been any travel to Earth or the Land of Whoo from any other portals. The answer was of course no, since he had given that direction. The portal added that after Princess Marie had arrived on Earth, it had been the custom every year since for the portals to send a messenger to check for any changes so they could track anyone who entered. People from other lands sometimes came to this portal room, but seeing no messages or changes, they would leave.

"Now, with your travels, there has been additional activity in the system. When those from other lands try to enter, they will be greeted by your message that entry is forbidden."

"Great point," said the Chosen One. "Can I record a message to be played when access is requested to either Earth or the Land of Whoo from a portal in other lands?"

"Yes, Master, please repeat your message so we may be prepared."

"This is Prince Michael Henry, the Chosen One. My mother was Princess Marie from the Land of Whoo and also Earth, and my father was Prince Knox of Whoo. We have just freed the Land of Whoo from the oppression of the Dark Wizard and the warlord Master Uror, and the kingdom is now at peace. I have restricted entry to Whoo and to Earth as a security precaution while we sort out our options. There will be no entry or exit allowed except for me and whomever accompanies me. We welcome peaceful coexistence with any other lands within or outside of our system. If you wish to discuss this further, please leave a message with the portal and a marker will be sent to me. I will reply at my earliest convenience. Do not try to force entry, as you will be turned away. We are at peace and we welcome you. Thank you for your interest."

With that the portal closed with a whir and reopened to report that the message had been saved, and that a marker would be available that the Eye of the Tiger could detect and relay to Michael Henry.

Though he had already sealed the portal, he did notice several of the portals light up as he shone his flashlight in their direction before they left. Ignoring his instinct to check things out, he continued down the path after Savannah.

The prince and Savannah rode their bikes to the farmhouse as he dispatched the Eye of the Tiger to check on his and Savannah's family. With all of his adventures, he had been thinking about his brother, Jeremy, a lot lately and also asked the Eye to check on him. The Chosen One said to check Whitworth University, where his brother was attending school.

Penny ran out to greet them. Though they had only been gone a short while in Earth time, she made them stop and pet her like she had not seen them for days. Her barking alerted GiGi, who also came out to greet them.

"Hi, GiGi, how are you feeling?" Savannah asked.

GiGi made them get off their bikes and gave them both a hug. She said quietly that she had the energy of a person half of her age and had started an aerobics class in Marysville. She had just returned from her first class and the instructor had marveled at her stamina and resting heart rate after strenuous exercise. She was indeed cured and better than before.

"Michael Henry, I have you and you alone to thank," she said. "I will never forget the day you cured me in the hospital."

"You're welcome, GiGi. My only reward is your silence and seeing you enjoy life once again."

"But why should I keep it silent? You deserve the credit, don't you, son?"

"I am concerned for my family as well. If the word got out about my powers before I was fully prepared to use them on Earth, some people with the wrong motivations

212

could use it against me and my family, putting them and you and Savannah in danger."

"Okay, mum's the word for now, Michael Henry."

Leslie and Paul came out to greet them, and Leslie invited Michael Henry for dinner. He declined, saying he should get home to check on things and see if his dad needed help with any projects. He took off down the lonely road. Just before he came to their street, he was greeted by the Eye of the Tiger.

"I have located your brother at Whitworth University outside of Spokane," said the Eye. "He seems to be doing just fine. Also, I dropped by your house, and your parents were having a disagreement about Jeremy's tuition and boarding expenses, your dad pushing for Whitworth because he graduated from there, but your mother pushing for a less expensive state school. Your dad wants to let Jeremy choose and says that even if they need to go into debt, he will work it out."

As Michael Henry rode up the driveway, he could see Mom and Dad through the window having a heated discussion. He entered noisily and slowly. When they saw him, their argument stopped and they welcomed him home.

"How was your day?" Sam asked, giving him a big hug.

"Great, Mom."

"Your dad and I are having a discussion about finances, just in case you overheard anything."

Michael Henry nodded. "What do you think about Jeremy going to Whitworth?" His dad said he thought it was a great idea and that he was working hard to provide for his family and allow his oldest son to attend the school of his choice.

"Where are you planning to go to college, Michael Henry?" Sam asked. He said he was not quite sure just yet, but that he would be interested in any of their ideas.

A ringing phone interrupted the conversation, and Dan answered. It was Providence Sacred Heart Medical Center and Children's Hospital in Spokane—Jeremy had been in a serious car accident and taken by ambulance to the ER. The highway patrol had found an ICE number on Jeremy's cell phone, and the hospital had called it looking for a relative.

"Give me the phone!" Sam cried. "I need to find out what is going on right now." Dan relinquished the phone to her as Michael Henry looked on. After a discussion that included medical terminology Michael Henry and Dan didn't understand, Sam finally hung up. "We need to get to Spokane as soon as we can," she said. Dan checked all available flights, and they headed for the airport. They made their flight and were across the state quickly. Once off the plane, Dan rented a car to drive to the hospital. On the way Sam related that the ER doctor, Dr. Roland, said that Jeremy had been seriously injured, and his chances of making it through the night were minimal. He had suffered a spinal cord injury and major head trauma and was in a coma. They were currently doing tests to determine his brain activity.

They pulled up to the hospital and parked the car. Dan took a deep breath. "Let's go see our oldest son." They checked in, found out where Jeremy was, and went to the intensive care unit. Sam sighed as she peered in at Jeremy, who seemed to be kept alive only by the machines he was hooked up to. Dr. Roland was there, and the family walked over to him with questions in their eyes.

The doctor introduced himself. "I wish I could be more hopeful," he said. "Jeremy has had a severe auto accident. I believe it is only because he was rushed to the ER within minutes of the accident that he is still holding on. You should know that even if he comes out of his coma, he will never be the same again and will be crippled for life. I only wish I could be more positive, but you deserve my honesty.

If it were my son, I would want to know exactly where I stood."

"Thank you, Dr. Roland, we appreciate your straightforward remarks," Dan said. Sam asked some specific medical questions but the answers were hard to hear.

Sam brushed Jeremy's hair fondly with her fingers as she spoke of her great love for him, saying she wanted him to know she was there for him. "Open your eyes, Jeremy," she pleaded. "Respond to your doctors."

Dan was next. He told Jeremy how much he meant to him. Thinking about how he wished he could relive their happy times, he spoke about how he was ready to take the boys fishing or camping or hiking.

Michael Henry looked at both of his parents and said, "I would like to spend some time alone with my brother. Can you go to the cafeteria and bring me back a sandwich?"

Sam nodded. "That would give us some time to talk, Dan." They headed out to the hospital cafeteria.

Now alone with his brother, Michael Henry laid his hand on Jeremy's head. "Jeremy, this is Michael Henry, the Chosen One. I have no malice toward any person or creature in the Land of Whoo or on Earth. I wish for you to be cured of your bodily illness. You will wake up and you will be fully cured." The prince felt a transfer of power from his hand to his brother's body, and then Jeremy woke up with a jolt.

"Hi, Jeremy," Michael Henry said with a smile. "Do you remember anything?" Jeremy shook his head no. The Chosen One pressed the call button and a nurse came in. Seeing that Jeremy was awake, she summoned her team to assess his condition.

Michael Henry texted his dad. "Jeremy just woke up."

Sam and Dan arrived out of breath. Sam immediately started talking with the nurses and looked at Jeremy's chart. "His vital signs are improving rapidly," she said. "Michael Henry, what did you say to him?"

He grinned. "I told him to wake up, of course."

The nurses buzzed around Jeremy and pointed to his vital signs, looking shocked.

"Jeremy, can you hear me, son?" Dan asked.

He answered slowly. "Yes, of course, Dad. How is my car?" They all laughed.

The night was uneventful. The nurses kept a close eye on Jeremy while Dan, Sam, and Michael Henry dozed in their chairs. The head nurse, Micki, told them that Jeremy was stable but needed some rest, so they would be better off in the waiting room or getting a hotel room for the night. They could return in the morning for the doctor's rounds. Micki promised to call Sam's cell phone if anything changed and urged them all to get some rest while Jeremy did the same.

"Okay, Micki," Dan agreed, and he led his family out of the hospital to find a nearby hotel for the rest of the night.

CHAPTER 21

A STRANGE MESSAGE
FROM THE PORTAL

Dan had set the alarm on his cell phone, and the family was up and ready to go by 6:15. They left their belongings in their room and had a quick free breakfast in the lobby. They went to the ICU but discovered that Jeremy had been moved to a regular room. They found him walking in the halls with a nurse by his side.

"Beat you to the door, bro," Michael Henry said, and they raced for Jeremy's room.

The nurse just beamed. "I can't believe how well he is doing," she said. Dr. Roland came down the hall and entered Jeremy's room. After seeing him and talking to him, the doctor came out to talk to the family.

"I have very good reason to hope for a full recovery. We are doing a series of tests this morning, and I just heard of his race with Michael Henry here. Even though we would not normally approve of that, your son shows remarkable signs of an amazing recovery. I will be back around noon to review his results."

"Dr. Roland, I want out of here," Jeremy called out from his bed. "When can I leave?"

"Let's complete these tests, and we'll discuss that when I return." The doctor then spoke privately with Dan and Sam. "I have never seen anything like this. I'm ordering some more tests, and then I will be able to give you an update. Right now I am very hopeful. He's had a 180-degree turnaround from yesterday."

Michael Henry walked down a hallway, sensing that the Eye of the Tiger had returned to give him an update. "All is well, Michael Henry. I even checked on Zack and Aaron and they are all one hundred percent, along with GiGi."

"What about Dr. Jordan? Has he given up his quest for information?"

"Let's face it: Dr. Jordan is a smart man. He will never fully accept what happened, but he remains thankful for the results and is planning to spend more time with his son."

"Great. I want you to make another flyby of all our families' houses and also the portal, just to be on the safe side."

Back in Jeremy's room, Dan, Sam, and Michael Henry waited for Jeremy's test results. Jeremy said that no one who had tested him could believe he was the same person that had been tested the night before – the results were so different. Finally Dr. Roland had reviewed all the tests and did a final exam of Jeremy's reflexes. He came out of Jeremy's room shaking his head. "I have never seen anything like this. Yesterday I would never have guessed that someone with such extensive injuries would ever be able to walk again, yet today he can run. Yesterday I would not have believed he would speak or recognize anyone again, or even be capable of responding in any way. Today he is asking for his phone to text his friends. I see no reason why he should not be released and return to his regular activities. He should come back for a follow-up with me in a month, unless he feels he needs to see me before that. Call for an appointment when you get home." He handed Sam his card.

The hospital staff all cheered as they left. Jeremy laughed as his brother wheeled him out in the mandatory wheelchair, trying to do wheelies. Dan went to get the rental car so they could take Jeremy back to his dorm. They stopped for lunch to celebrate and then headed back to Whitworth. As soon as they were on campus, Jeremy saw his friends and yelled at them out of the open car window. His friends ran over.

Michael Henry was bored as they stood around the car talking, so he texted Savannah. "Jeremy is fine. We will be back tonight - see you tomorrow. K?"

Savannah texted back, "Okay! GiGi wants to make cookies for us."

They parked and walked Jeremy back to his dorm. Michael Henry sensed the Eye of the Tiger heading his way and slipped behind some trees.

"Greetings," the prince said quietly. "What have you discovered, my friend?"

"As you remember, you gave specific instructions for the portal to notify you via a marker if anyone from another land wanted to visit Earth or the Land of Whoo. A moment ago, the portal received a message from a faraway land that King Vincent has requested an immediate audience."

Michael Henry asked the Eye what he knew of the request.

The Eye responded that the message was specifically from the Land of the Coral Seas and was marked as extremely urgent, for Michael Henry only.

Michael Henry looked off for a minute.

"And how should I reply, Eye of the Tiger?"

Made in the USA
Charleston, SC
15 November 2012